THE ESCORT

SANDI LYNN

THE ESCORT

New York Times, USA Today & Wall Street Journal
Bestselling Author
Sandi Lynn

The Escort

Copyright © 2019 Sandi Lynn Romance, LLC

All rights reserved. No part of this publication may be reproduced, distributed, or transmitted in any form or by any means, including photocopying, recording, or other electronic or mechanical methods without the prior written permission of the publisher.
This is a work of fiction. Names, characters, places and incidents are the products of the authors imagination or are used fictitiously. Any resemblance to actual events, locales, or persons, living or dead, is entirely coincidental.

Cover Design by Shanoff Designs

Editing by BZ Hercules

❦ Created with Vellum

MISSION STATEMENT

Sandi Lynn Romance

Providing readers with romance novels that will whisk them away to another world and from the daily grind of life – one book at a time.

1

Brielle

I walked into the Warwick Hotel in my black stiletto heels and short black dress. My eyes were covered behind large round black sunglasses, which complemented my long dark wavy hair, and my lips, which were painted a cherry red. The lobby was quite busy this afternoon, and as I strolled up to the front desk, I was greeted pleasantly by Joseph, one of the clerks that had known me for the past five years.

"Good afternoon, Emmy." He began typing away at his computer. "Should I just charge the card that's on file?"

"Good afternoon, Joseph. Always." I smiled.

"Your key, Madame." He handed me the card. "Enjoy your stay."

I gave him a small smile as I took the elevator up to the thirtieth floor, slid my key card, and opened the door to the room I considered my second home: room 3010. After throwing my purse on the bed, I set my bag down and went into the bathroom to check myself one last time before my client arrived. There was a light knock at the door, and when I opened it, a man who was in his mid-forties and stood approximately five foot eight with short black hair and a light mustache nervously stood there.

"Hi, I'm Emmy. You must be Lawrence." I smiled.

"Nice to meet you, Emmy."

"Come in and make yourself comfortable." I gestured with my hand.

He stepped inside the room and looked around. His hands were fidgeting, and I could tell he was a nervous wreck.

"First time?" I asked to try and ease his nervousness.

"Yes." He turned and looked at me.

"How about a drink?" I asked as I walked over to the mini-bar.

"Sure. Got any bourbon?"

"Of course." I lightly smiled as I poured him a glass. "So, Lawrence, how do you like being a dentist?"

He answered my question and we made small talk. I always liked to have a conversation with my new clients first to ease into what was to come next. He sat on the edge of the bed while I slipped out of my dress. I could see the beads of sweat form on his forehead. I hoped to god this guy wasn't going to have a heart attack on me. I knelt down between his legs and softly brushed my lips against his, testing the waters, so to speak. He paid extra for kissing, so I needed to be sure he really wanted it. His hands nervously roamed to my breasts, which were covered by a black lace push-up bra.

"You're a very beautiful woman, Emmy."

"And you're a very sexy man, Lawrence," I spoke as my fingers unbuckled his belt.

After undoing his pants, I slid my hand down the front of them and grabbed hold of his semi-hard cock, stroking it softly and feeling it harden in my hand. He let out a moan and then grabbed my hand and pushed it away.

"I'm sorry. I'm so sorry. I don't think I can go through with this."

I sighed as I stood up and then sat down next to him, placing my hand on his thigh.

"Why don't you tell me what's going on at home that drove you to contact me in the first place?"

"I love my wife. I really do. We've been married for fifteen years and haven't had sex in over a year. She's always tired, never feeling well, the kids drive her crazy, and we grew apart. I hate that it happened to us. We're both so busy all the time between our jobs and the kids. Emmy, I'm starving for sex. A man can only take care of himself for so long. But despite all of our problems, I don't think I can cheat on her. I thought I could come here, have a fun time with you, and go home. But the reality is, we haven't done anything, and I already feel guilty."

"Listen, Lawrence. I love that you love your wife, and you should. You have a beautiful family and so many wonderful memories. What you need to do is reignite your passion with her. Take her on a date. Get someone to watch the kids and go away for a long weekend. I can guarantee that if you make her a priority and forget everything else for a minute, the two of you will be having sex again. You two just need to rediscover what it's like to be a couple in love. When was the last time you bought her flowers for absolutely no reason?"

"I don't know. Years, I guess."

"Then start there. When you leave here, stop at the florist, buy the prettiest flowers they have, take them home to her, and tell her how much you love her. Arrange for someone to watch the kids and take her to dinner. Don't tell her about it. Just do it."

He placed his hand on mine and gave it a gentle squeeze.

"Thank you, Emmy. I'm going to do just that. I'm sorry that I wasted your time."

"You didn't waste my time, Lawrence. Just remember that my fee is non-refundable."

"I know." He smiled as he stood up, reached into his wallet, and pulled out a hundred-dollar bill. "I know I already paid, but here's a little something extra for being so cool about all this."

I took the money from his hand, stood up, wrapped my arms around his neck, and kissed his cheek.

"Thank you. You're a good man, Lawrence, and your wife is very lucky to have you."

After he left the hotel room, I changed into a pair of ripped jeans, a long-sleeved black shirt, and my black Converse. Grabbing my phone, I sent a text message to Ben.

"I'm leaving the hotel in about five minutes."

"I'll be waiting, Brielle."

I grabbed my purse and my bag, put on my sunglasses, and walked out the door. Once I reached the lobby, I made my way to the front desk to check out.

"Let me guess, he couldn't go through with it?" Joseph smirked.

"No. He couldn't." I smiled.

"Enjoy the rest of your day, Emmy."

"You too, Joseph."

I walked out the doors of the lobby and climbed into the back of the sedan.

"That was quick." Ben smiled as he glanced back at me.

"He was feeling guilty. I sort of felt bad for the guy," I said as I took off my wig and pulled my long blonde hair back in a ponytail and placed a black Nike cap on.

I removed my green-colored contacts and placed them in their case as well as my false eyelashes. Taking the makeup remover wipes from my bag, I cleansed my face.

"Where to? Home?" Ben asked.

"No. I want to go to the shooting range for a while."

"You got it, boss."

Ben Riley had been my driver and one of my best friends for the past four years. He was a handsome guy who stood six foot four, black hair that he kept in a buzz cut, and a full beard and mustache that he always kept neatly trimmed. We met in a coffee shop when our coffees got switched. He grabbed mine and I grabbed his. Luckily, neither one of us had left yet. We exchanged coffees and got to talking. It turned out he had just lost his job as a driver to an influential family in New York City and was on the hunt for one. It just so happened that I had been thinking about hiring someone to drive me to and from my jobs. It was a win/win for both of us. He was a part-time artist who loved to paint and sculpt things. Unfortunately, what he did wasn't bringing in much money, so he depended on another part-time job to fill in the gap. It didn't take too long for us to become friends. He was my confidant and I could talk to him about anything.

Ben pulled up to the curb of the shooting range and I climbed out of the car.

"I'll only be about an hour," I said.

"I'll be waiting for you." He smiled.

I walked inside and saw Jimmy standing behind the counter.

"Hey, Jimmy."

"Hi, Brielle. Haven't seen you in a couple of weeks."

"Life, Jimmy. Life." I smiled as he reached under the counter and handed me my box.

Taking my lane, I put on my protective glasses and my earmuffs. Ejecting the magazine from my 9mm Glock 43 Caliber, I loaded it with bullets, disengaged the safety lever, aligned my eye with the target, and began firing.

"Damn, Brielle," Jimmy spoke. "God help anyone who pisses you off."

I gave him a smile as I stared at the six bullet holes that were perfect shots. After practicing for about an hour with moving targets, I unloaded my gun, packed up, and headed home.

"Have a good day, Jimmy. I'll see you next week."

"Looking forward to it, Brielle."

I'd been going to the shooting range to practice for the past five years. Being a twenty-seven-year-old woman alone in New York City and in my profession, I needed to protect myself. In case you haven't already figured it out, I'm an escort. Not just any escort, but a self-employed high-end escort. The men who acquired my services were generally the wealthy ones. Doctors, lawyers, hedge fund managers, CEOs, dentists, etc. You get the picture. Ninety percent of my clients were married. The other ten percent were those who had no interest in dating a woman but needed sex.

2

Brielle

When I was growing up, I never in a million years thought that I would become an escort. It wasn't who I was. I was a bright and intelligent girl who got straight A's throughout school, graduated as class valedictorian, scored the highest number on the SATs, and got a full ride scholarship to any college I wanted. I didn't come from money. My mother was a single parent who worked two jobs, sometimes three, to try and make ends meet, and it still wasn't enough. We lived in a tiny one-bedroom apartment where my mother slept on the couch.

When I was eighteen, and right before I was scheduled to attend NYU, my mother was diagnosed with cancer and had to undergo many rounds of chemotherapy. Because she was so ill and missed a lot of work, she was fired and lost the shitty health insurance she had right before she was diagnosed. I had to put college on the back burner so I could get a job and take care of her. The problem was, the job I got waitressing didn't pay shit, even with the tips. She was getting further behind in her bills. Not only her everyday living expenses, but also the high medical bills that were rolling in. We were on the verge of getting evicted. I did the best I could, but it was never enough and we were both sinking fast.

One night, I ran into a woman named Marie who was having dinner with some people at the restaurant I worked at. When she stepped outside to have a cigarette, she saw me crying. She walked over and asked me if I was okay. I tried to play it off as if it were nothing, but she knew better. She got me to talk about my situation, and after she heard my story, she offered me some help. She told me how she was an escort and that she was getting ready to retire from it, but she didn't want to leave her clients high and dry. She said I was a beautiful woman and asked me if I'd be interested in trying it out. I'll never forget what she said.

"Listen, darling, you'll make more money in one month than you do for an entire year working at this place."

I didn't have a choice at the time, and I knew it would only be temporary until my mother and I could get back on our feet. She coached me, taught me the ropes, and when I was ready, she sent me some of her clients. I hated it, but I loved the money. These men paid me well, which allowed me to pay off my mother's medical bills and help us get back on our feet.

I escorted for two and a half years before I decided to get out of the business because of a man named Daniel. He was, or so I thought, the love of my life and swept me off my feet from the moment he looked at me. We dated for a month and trying to hide what I did for a living was difficult. As far as he was concerned, I worked as a home health aide with crazy hours. So I quit and ended up getting an office job as a receptionist working 9-5. We dated for about six months and I was happy. Happier than I'd ever been, until I got pregnant. The night I told him, he asked me if I was going to keep the baby. I was shocked that he would even ask such a question. When I told him yes, he hugged me and told me he was happy too. That same night, he went out to get us food and I never saw him again.

I gave birth to Stella when I was twenty-one years old. The company I worked for ended up closing its doors when I was on maternity leave. I took some time off looking for another job because I didn't know what I was going to do with Stella, and needless to say, the little nest egg I had saved from my escorting days ran out quickly between living expenses, hospital bills, and schooling expenses.

As I sat holding her in my arms and stared down at her precious face, I knew I wanted to give her everything she deserved. She didn't ask to be born and she didn't deserve her father abandoning her. I wanted a better life for my daughter than what I had, so I knew what I had to do. Only this time, it would be different.

Once my mother went into remission and was cancer free, she got a job as a secretary in a real estate office. She worked the normal 9-5 hours and made barely enough to support herself and help me out. I could change that for her. So after having a long conversation, she agreed to quit and take care of Stella while I worked. This time around, my job wasn't the couple of hours here and there. Sometimes it consisted of two, maybe three-day weekends. But that was where I drew the line. I was never gone more than three days at a time. And when I came home, I didn't work for three days so I could spend all of my time with Stella.

My mother knew what I did for work. We never kept secrets from each other. And even though she didn't like me getting back into escorting, she knew I had to do what was best for Stella. Plus, she liked the money I paid her and the apartment I put her up in.

*

"Mommy." Stella smiled as she ran into my arms. Picking her up, I hugged her tight.

"Hello, baby. How was school?" I asked as I put her down.

"Fine."

"Just 'fine'?" I patted her head as we walked to the car.

"It was kind of boring. Hi, Ben." Her face lit up.

"Hello, little lady." He grinned.

We climbed into the back of the car and Ben shut the door and drove us home.

"Take your backpack to your room," I said as we stepped inside. "What do you want for dinner?"

"Surprise me," she said as she took off down the hallway.

I walked to my office, where I found my friend and personal assistant, Sasha, sitting behind her desk.

"How did it go?" she asked as she looked up from her computer.

"He couldn't go through with it, so we just talked. I told him to take his wife on a date and buy her some flowers."

Sasha let out a laugh.

"I'll flag his account in case he wants to book you again," she said.

"Good idea, but I don't think he will."

"Mr. Willows called and booked you for next weekend. Friday-Sunday. He has an event in Texas he needs to attend. He's flying you out Friday morning and you'll be back Sunday night."

"Good. I like Texas." I smiled. "Are you staying for dinner?"

"No. Not tonight. I'm teaching yoga over at the studio. In fact," she glanced at her watch, "I better get going."

"Stella, Auntie Sasha is leaving. Come say goodbye," I shouted down the hallway.

Stella came running in and hugged Sasha goodbye.

"You're not staying for dinner?" Stella pouted.

"Not tonight, missy. I have a yoga class to teach."

Sasha Hathaway and I had been friends since junior high school. She was there for me when my mom was sick and she was there for me with Stella. Not only was she one of my best friends, she was my personal assistant and helped out with Stella from time to time. As far as anyone outside my little circle was concerned, I was a freelance marketing consultant. After Daniel left me, I took some college classes in marketing with the hopes of moving up in the company I had worked for. Little did I know they'd go under and it would become my perfect cover.

3

Brielle

The clients who hired me always saw me in disguise. Long brown hair, emerald-green eyes, and a face full of makeup. Never did I allow any of my clients to see my true self. The last thing I needed was for them to recognize me on the street. Plus, it was safer that way. I also never allowed them to know my real name: Brielle Winters. They only knew me as Emmy Pine. When you're in the kind of business I am, you have connections. Connections that allowed me to obtain a fake ID, credit cards, and bank accounts in my escort name.

☙

"Now you be good for Grandma." I smiled as I brushed a strand of Stella's hair out of her face.

"I always am." She grinned.

"I love you and I'll see you in a couple of days." I hugged her tight.

"I love you too, Mommy."

"Have a safe trip, honey," my mom spoke as she hugged me.

"Thanks, Mom."

I grabbed my suitcase and my bag, headed out the door and down to the lobby where Ben was waiting for me. As I sat in the back of the car, I did my makeup and put on my wig. Every time I left Stella, I felt a pain in my heart.

"Have a safe trip, Brielle. I'll be here when you get back."

"Thanks, Ben. I'll see you in a couple of days." I smiled as I climbed out and he shut the door behind me.

Walking into the airport, I checked in, made it through security, and took my seat in first class, compliments of Derek Willows. He had been a long-time client of mine. Four years to be exact. He was the CEO of Willow Vineyards in California. We met when I was out there with another client of mine. I was convenient for him and only saw him when he traveled. He was mid-fifties, six feet tall, salt and pepper hair that was perfectly kept and brown eyes. He and his wife Trish had been married for twenty-five years and they had four children. I was his escape. Something he desperately craved. We had become close friends over the past four years. He could talk to me about things he couldn't with his wife and that took some of the pressure off him. That was what most of my clients told me. It just wasn't always about the sex. A majority of the time, it was about understanding and just being there to listen to them.

When I arrived in Texas, there was a car waiting for me to take me to the Rosewood Manor on Turtle Creek hotel. When I walked into the lobby, I saw Derek standing there, looking dapper in his designer navy blue suit.

"Hello, darling." He smiled as he took my hands and kissed my cheek.

"Hello, Derek." I returned his smile.

He took my suitcase and my bag from me and we took the elevator up to his suite.

"Nice," I said as I looked around. "So how's Trish doing?"

"She's Trish," he spoke as he walked over to the bar and poured me a glass of red wine. "Devon moved out and now it's just the two of us in that big house. So you can imagine how things are. It's like we don't even know each other anymore. Anyway, how are you?"

"I'm good." I smiled.

"Business going good?" he asked.

"Yes. Business is really good."

"Good. I'm happy to hear that. Tonight's event is formal, so there's a dress I rented for you hanging in the closet along with some jewelry in a box on the dresser."

"Thank you, Derek."

He took the glass from my hand and set it on the table. Bringing his hand up to my face, he softly kissed my lips.

"It's been quite a while since I've had sex, so I've been looking forward to this since I booked you."

After our romp in the sack, he ordered room service for us and we chatted about what was going on in his life and his business before we were to attend the event. While he showered, I touched up my makeup and ran a brush through my brown hair. After slipping into the strapless black form-fitted dress that was hanging in the closet, Derek took the diamond necklace from the box and slipped it around my neck.

"You look as beautiful as always, Emmy."

"And you look as handsome as always." I smiled as I straightened his bow tie.

The thing with these business events was I was never the only escort in the room. These types of men always brought escorts with them while their wives sat at home. They had a guy code: I won't tell if you won't.

The event was being held outside in the garden area, which was astoundingly beautiful. Waiters and waitresses carrying around trays of champagne and hor d'oeuvres were dressed in black form-fitting suits. Round tables that seated eight were set up with fine white linen and china.

"Derek, it's good to see you," a devilishly handsome man said as he approached.

"Caden. How are you? I didn't know you were going to be here."

"It was a last-minute thing," he spoke as his eyes raked over me. "Is she with you?"

"Yes, forgive me. Caden, this is Emmy. Emmy, this is Caden Chamberlain."

"It's a pleasure to meet you." He slyly smiled as he extended his hand.

"And you as well, Mr. Chamberlain."

His fingers wrapped around my hand as his eyes stared into mine. A few moments later, everyone was called to take their seats.

"We're at table fourteen," Derek spoke.

"So am I." Caden grinned.

Derek and I took our seats and Caden sat on the other side of me. I wasn't going to lie and tell you that I felt comfortable, because I didn't. Mr. Chamberlain made me very uncomfortable. I didn't know if it was the way he stared at me with a hunger in his eyes or the fact that he was one hell of a sexy man. He was approximately thirty years old and stood six foot two with sassy light brown hair. He kept it shorter on the sides and a medium length on top, which was swept up, giving him an edgy look. He had a masculine jaw line, which sported a neatly kept five o'clock shadow, chiseled cheekbones, and deep blue eyes. I'd seen many men in my time, but no one that had ever caught my attention the way Caden Chamberlain had.

After dinner, and before the guest speakers took their turn, I got up from my seat and headed into the hotel to use the ladies' room. When I was finished, I couldn't find Derek anywhere, so I went over to the bar to get a drink.

"What can I get for you?" the bartender asked.

"I'll have a gin martini, neat, with a twist of lemon."

"Excellent choice," I heard a voice say next to me.

When I glanced over, I saw Caden leaning up against the bar with a smile on his face.

"Thank you."

"I'll have the same except no lemon," he spoke to the bartender.

"You haven't by any chance seen Derek, have you?" I asked.

"His phone rang, and he walked away to take the call. I haven't seen him since. Did he hire you to spend the weekend with him?"

The bartender set our drinks down and I quickly grabbed my glass and brought it up to my lips.

"That's something you'll have to ask him yourself," I replied.

He stood there with his drink in his hand and narrowed his eye at me.

"I don't have to ask him. I already know because there's no way someone as gorgeous as you would hook up with that old geezer unless you were getting paid."

I raised my brow at him as I sipped my martini.

"There you are." Derek ran over to me in a panic. "I'm sorry, but I have to get back to California. Trish had a heart attack and they're taking her into emergency surgery."

"Oh my god, Derek. I'm so sorry."

"If anything happens to her, Emmy."

I reached out and grabbed hold of his hand.

"She's going to be okay, Derek."

"Caden, when are you leaving here?" he asked him.

"Tomorrow morning. Why?"

"Can Emmy fly with you back to New York?"

"That's okay, Derek. I'll book a flight."

"No," Caden spoke. "You're more than welcome to fly back with me on my private jet."

"It's fine. I'll pull up the flights now." I reached in my purse and pulled out my phone.

"I said you're flying back with me," he spoke in an authoritative tone. "There's no sense in paying for a ticket change when you can fly absolutely free."

"Thank you, Caden. I have to run. Emmy, I'll be in touch, darling."

4

Caden

She was one hell of a sexy woman, and the only thing I could think about was being buried deep inside her. My cock throbbed at the mere sight of her. She finished her drink, grabbed her purse, and got up from the bar stool.

"It was nice to meet you, Mr. Chamberlain, but I think I'm going to call it a night."

"How much?" I asked.

"Excuse me?"

"How much for the night? The entire night?"

"I'm sorry, but I don't work that way."

"What's the name of your agency? I'll call them now and book you since there was a change in your plans."

"I don't work for an agency, Mr. Chamberlain. I work for myself."

"Better yet." I smirked. "Spend the night with me and I'll pay you twenty thousand dollars."

"Twenty thousand dollars for one night?" Her brow raised.

"Yes, because I get the feeling you'll be worth every penny."

"Have you ever hired an escort before?" she asked.

"No. I don't need to. I can have any woman I want at any time."

"Then go find yourself one. There's no sense in paying for sex when you can get it for free." She slyly smiled at me as she walked away.

I threw back my drink and set the glass down on the bar.

"Meet me at the restaurant terrace tomorrow morning at nine a.m. and we'll have breakfast together before we get on my plane and head back to New York. At least let me buy you breakfast."

She stopped, turned around, and stared at me for a moment.

"I'll tell you what, I'll meet you for breakfast, but it's on me. It's the least I can do since you're letting me fly home for free. Deal?" she asked with an arch in her brow.

"Okay then. Deal."

I watched her walk away and step into the elevator. Her five-foot-seven slender body was sculpted to perfection. Judging by the way her cleavage looked in that dress, I would guess she was a natural C cup. All I needed was a little patience and soon enough my lips would be all over those beautiful breasts of hers and my cock would be feeling the warmth of her pussy.

Brielle

I stepped into the suite and kicked off my shoes. Who the hell was I to turn down twenty thousand dollars for one night with a man like Caden Chamberlain? I was stupid, nuts, and certifiably crazy. Derek paid me a total of twenty-five thousand for the weekend. So if I would have taken Mr. Chamberlain up on his offer, I would have walked away with a total of forty-five thousand dollars in my pocket. But I couldn't. I wasn't breaking my rule and potentially putting myself in danger. Plus, there was something about him that was taboo, and I couldn't quite put my finger on it. I had good instincts and my instincts told me that if I would have spent the night with him without proper procedure, I would have regretted it.

I went into the bathroom to start a bath when I heard a knock at the door. Looking out the peephole, I saw it was Caden. *Shit. What the fuck was he doing here?* A nervousness settled inside me, so I went back to the bedroom, retrieved my gun from my bag and quickly loaded it just in case. Walking to the door, I placed my hand on the handle, stood behind it, and slowly opened it.

"Emmy?" he spoke as he stepped inside.

Cocking the gun, I pointed it to the back of his head.

"Put your hands up and slowly turn around," I spoke.

"Holy shit. Are you pointing a gun to my head?"

He did as I asked and slowly turned around.

"How did you know what room I was in?"

"I asked the front desk which room was Derek's because you left your phone on the bar downstairs. It's in the left pocket of my jacket. Feel free to get it yourself."

With the gun still pointed at him, I reached into his pocket and grabbed my phone.

"Thank you," I said.

"You're welcome. I can see you're overly cautious and that's great. You should be. But do you think you can put that thing down? It's making me really nervous. Please." He begged.

I put the safety back on and lowered my gun.

"Thank you." He let out a deep breath. "I will say you are the first person ever to point a gun at me." The corners of his mouth curved upwards.

"A woman can never be too careful."

"Hey, I totally agree." He put his hand up. "Anyway, I just came here to give your phone back. I'll see you on the terrace tomorrow morning. Have a good night."

"You too, Mr. Chamberlain."

"Please, just call me Caden."

Caden

Damn, she didn't play around. My heart was still beating out of my chest. But I wasn't sure if it was from the fact that she could have shot me or that she looked incredibly sexy pointing that gun at me. I went back to my suite and poured myself a drink. I couldn't stop thinking about her, and the moment we got back to New York, she'd be mine for one night.

5

Brielle

As I sat in the warm, bubbly tub, I sent my mom a text message.

"Change of plans. I'm coming home tomorrow instead of Sunday."

"Why? What happened?"

"His wife had a heart attack and he needed to leave."

"Oh dear. I hope she's okay."

"Me too, Mom. Tell Stella I love her and I'll be home tomorrow."

After I finished texting her, I sent a message to Ben letting him know of my change of plans.

As soon as I finished my bath, I put on the fluffy white robe in the closet and sat down at the computer to find out more about Caden Chamberlain. He was thirty years old, just as I suspected and was the President of Chamberlain Essence, a billion-dollar flavoring company. His status was single, and he was one of New York's most eligible bachelors. Clicking on the images tab, I found there were several pictures with him and a string of women on his arm.

"You are quite the playboy, Mr. Chamberlain," I said as I logged off the computer and went to bed.

The next morning, I showered, put on my wig, my colored contacts, a face full of makeup, and dressed in a pair of ripped jeans and a tank top. Grabbing my purse, I headed out the door and to the terrace to meet Caden for breakfast. When I arrived, I saw him sitting at a table, so I walked over and took the seat across from him.

"Good morning." He smiled.

"Good morning."

"Coffee?" He reached for the small stainless steel pot that sat on the table.

"Please."

"How did you sleep last night?" he asked.

"I slept good. How about you?"

"Not so good. All I kept seeing when I closed my eyes was a gun pointed at me." He smirked.

"Again, I'm sorry about that."

"My plane has already arrived, so we can head to the airport as soon as we're finished with breakfast."

"Sounds good."

"By the way, Emmy. What is your last name?" he asked as he sipped his coffee.

"Why?" I gave him a smirk.

"I have an event next Saturday night that I have to attend, and I would like to hire you to go with me."

"Why?" I narrowed my eye at him.

"Because I think you're a beautiful woman and I'd like your company. Good enough reason?"

"But you can have any woman you want for free."

"True. But I'd like to take you."

"I'm already booked for next Saturday night."

"Cancel the booking. I'll pay triple your rate and I promise I'll be much better company than the old geezer who booked you."

"And how do you know he's an old geezer?" I cocked my head.

"Because I don't think there are too many thirty-year-olds who hire escorts. Am I right?"

"Yes. I suppose so. He's a new client, though."

"Good. Then it'll be even easier to cancel." He grinned.

"You have to go through a screening process first."

"No problem. I want you for the entire night. You can leave the next morning."

"I'm assuming you want sex," I said as I sipped my coffee.

"You assumed right." He winked. "And a couple other things."

"Twenty thousand," I spoke.

The corners of his mouth curved upwards into a sly smile.

"I know damn well you don't charge that."

"You were willing to pay that last night," I said with an arch in my brow.

"Fine. Twenty thousand dollars for the night and you're all mine."

I reached into my purse and pulled out my business card.

"Call the number on the card, go through the proper channels, and I'll make sure I'm available that night."

After breakfast, I went up to my hotel suite to grab my luggage. Pulling my phone from my purse, I called Sasha.

"Hey, Brielle. How's Texas?"

"Eventful to say the least. I'm going to be heading home today. Derek's wife had a heart attack and he needed to leave last night."

"That sucks. I hope she's okay."

"Listen, I need you to cancel my appointment for next Saturday with that new client. A gentleman by the name of Caden Chamberlain is going to be calling to hire me for that night. I've already met him here in Texas. Screen him anyway. He wants me for the entire night and he's paying me twenty thousand dollars."

"Holy shit. For one night? How did you manage that?"

"He was willing to pay it last night after Derek left and I turned him down. He really wants to spend the night with me, so I told him twenty grand and he agreed."

"Damn, Brielle."

"He's the president of a billion-dollar flavoring company. Twenty thousand is pennies to him."

"Umm, Brielle. I just googled his name. He's thirty years old and he's fucking hot as hell. Shit. I'd let him fuck me for free."

I let out a light laugh. "If we had met when I was Brielle and not on the job, I probably would have."

"Gotta go, the other line is ringing. It's probably him. Have a safe flight."

I ended the call, grabbed my suitcase, and headed to the lobby where Caden was waiting for me and talking on the phone. After he ended the call, he looked at me.

"Damn, you put new clients through an ordeal."

"Like I said, a woman needs to protect herself." I smiled as we climbed into the back of his limo.

6

Caden

"I can take you home if you need a ride," I spoke as the plane landed.

"I have a car waiting for me. But thanks for the offer."

We unbuckled our seatbelts, grabbed our luggage, and exited the plane.

"I would like to have your number in case I need to speak to you before Saturday."

"Only regular clients get my number."

"I see. And who's to say I won't become a regular client? But I am paying you twenty thousand dollars for one night, so I think that should include a phone number."

"You think so?" She cocked her head.

"I do. We have entered into a business arrangement and usually phone numbers are exchanged."

"Okay then."

I pulled out my phone and entered the number she rattled off.

"Thank you. I'll see you next Saturday." I smiled.

"Are you not going to give me your number?" she asked.

"I'll be in touch." I gave her a wink.

"Okay then, see you next Saturday."

I watched her as she walked away, rolling her suitcase behind her. I followed her into the airport, keeping my distance so she didn't see me. She went into the bathroom and I waited at the Starbucks across the way for her to come out. I stood there in shock when she walked out.

"I'll be damned," I whispered to myself.

She was no longer a brunette, but a blonde. A very sexy and beautiful blonde-haired woman. She disguised herself for her clients. Smart woman. I pulled her card out of my pocket and stared at her name: Emmy Pine. I would guarantee that was fake as well.

I headed home to my Park Avenue penthouse. When I stepped off the elevator, I left my suitcase in the foyer and walked over to the bar and poured myself a drink. Taking it out to the balcony, I leaned over the railing and thought about her. I thought she was sexy as a brunette, but after seeing her as a blonde, it took my excitement to a whole other level. Now she was more of a mystery and I was going to find out exactly who she was. I finished my drink, set my glass down, and headed out of my building to go see my brother Kyle. He was the founder and owner of Upscale, a fine dining five-star restaurant in the Financial District.

"Good evening, Mr. Chamberlain."

"Good evening, Allison. Where's my brother?"

"In the kitchen." She smiled flirtatiously at me.

The place was packed like it always was. To get in, you had to make reservations at least two months in advance. My brother was an excellent chef, which had been his passion since he was a kid. He tried the family business and it made him miserable. The only thing that made him happy was being in a kitchen. He wasn't an office, sit-behind-a-desk type of guy. He was my older brother by three years, and he was also my best friend.

"Hey bro. Nice surprise." He grinned as I walked into the kitchen.

"Hey." I grabbed a bacon-wrapped scallop from the aluminum pan sitting on the counter.

"You're just in time. I was going to take a break. Did you eat?"

"No. Not yet."

"Marcus, put a plate together for me and Caden and bring it in back," he spoke.

"Sure thing, boss."

We walked to the small room off the side, which was where parties were held. Taking a seat at a table, Kyle handed me a bourbon.

"Thanks."

"How was Texas?" he asked as he took the seat across from me.

"I was there one day, and it was eventful to say the least." I arched my brow as I took a sip of my drink.

"Eventful in a good way or a bad way?"

"Depends on how you look at it. I met a woman at the hotel and there was something about her that caught my attention very quickly."

"Like?"

"She was sexy, poised, smart. Someone I wanted to fuck very badly."

"I take it you didn't?"

"No. She turned down my offer."

"Offer?" His brows furrowed.

"I offered to pay her twenty thousand dollars for the night."

He chuckled as Marcus set our plates down in front of us. "What is she, an escort or something?"

"Yeah. She is. She was with Derek Willows and he had to fly out due to a family emergency."

"You're serious, aren't you?"

"Dead serious."

"Why the fuck would she turn down twenty grand, and why didn't you just call her agency?"

"She doesn't work for an agency. She works for herself. She has a screening process that all clients have to go through first. Wait, it gets better." I smiled. "She left her phone on the bar, so I went up to the suite she was in to give it back to her. The door opened and I didn't see her, so I stepped inside. That was when she pointed a gun to the back of my head."

"Oh my god." He laughed. "What did she think? You were going to rape her or something?"

"I guess so, since she had a gun pointed at me. I explained to her that I was only there to give her back her phone, which she left down at the bar."

"She sounds like a psycho."

"She's not. She was being cautious, and I admire that. It made her sexier in my eyes." I smirked. "Anyway, she lives here in New York and I offered her a ride back on my jet. She accepted and I've hired her to attend an event with me on Saturday night."

"At what cost?" His brow raised.

"Twenty thousand."

He sat across from me and slowly shook his head.

"You're seriously going to pay her twenty grand for the night?"

"Yes. I am. I know she'll be worth every penny. I can feel it."

"Are you bored or something? There are women lining up all over the city trying to sleep with you for free and you're going to pay some escort?"

"I can't figure it out myself. All I know is there's something about her that intrigues me. Anyway, it's only one night. Once I fuck her, I'll get her out of my system and send her on her way."

"Good luck, brother. I hope she's worth the money."

7

SATURDAY

Brielle

I was making breakfast for Stella when my business cell phone rang with a number I didn't recognize. I declined the call and a text message came through.

"It's Caden Chamberlain. I'm going to call you again. Make sure you answer. I need to talk to you about tonight."

A moment later, it rang again, so I answered it.

"Hello, Mr. Chamberlain."

"Hello, Emmy," his low voice spoke.

"If you're calling to cancel—"

"No. I'm not cancelling. I have a request for tonight."

"And what is that?" I asked.

"I don't want you to wear your wig. I want you to come as your natural self. Not in disguise."

"Excuse me?" I started to tremble.

"I saw you come out of the bathroom in the airport and your hair was blonde. I would imagine your eye color was fake as well as the brunette wig you wore. I want the real you tonight. Plus, there are going to be a lot of high class, influential, and wealthy people at this event and I'm sure someone will recognize you if you're in costume.

Truth be told, I really don't want anyone to know that I'm bringing an escort as a date."

Shit. Shit. Shit. What the fuck was I going to do?

"I'm sorry, Mr. Chamberlain, but I only work in disguise. If you're embarrassed that someone will see you with me, then maybe we should just cancel our date."

"No," he abruptly spoke. "Thirty thousand."

"What? Are you crazy?"

"Perhaps I am. Come as yourself and I will pay you thirty thousand for tonight. If you're worried, don't be. I already know you'll be bringing your gun and I really don't feel like being threatened with it again."

"I have to go. I'm in the middle of something. Let me give it some thought, and I'll get back with you."

"You have two hours, Miss Pine."

I ended the call and took in a deep breath. There was a knock at the door and I jumped. Placing my hand over my heart, I unlocked it and Sasha walked in.

"Good morning. I need coffee bad. Please tell me some is made."

"There's a full pot. I need to talk to you about something, but not in front of Stella."

"Sure. Okay. Where is she?"

"In her room. But her breakfast is ready. Stella?" I shouted. "Breakfast is ready."

She came running into the kitchen in her jammies and wrapped her arms around Sasha's legs.

"Good morning, princess," Sasha spoke as leaned down and kissed the top of her head.

"Are you staying for breakfast?" Stella asked her.

"Of course. It's not that often I get to have breakfast with my favorite girl."

I set a plate of waffles in the middle of the table and grabbed another plate for Sasha.

"Don't forget you're spending the night at Grandma's. Mommy has to work."

"I know. Grandma said she'd play Monopoly with me tonight." She grinned.

"Awesome." I smiled as I got up from the table and poured some more coffee into my cup.

As soon as she was done eating, I told her to go get dressed and I'd take her to Central Park for a while.

"What's going on?" Sasha asked as soon as Stella left the table.

"Caden Chamberlain called me right before you got here. Apparently, he saw me come out of the bathroom at the airport without my wig on."

"Shit. Was he following you or something?"

"I don't know. He must have been. Anyway, he wants me to come tonight out of disguise and he said he'll pay me thirty grand if I do."

"Shit, Brielle. What are you going to do? I mean, for thirty grand, I think you should. What's the harm? He already saw you. So if you run into him on the street, he'll know who you are anyway."

"I don't know."

"There shouldn't be a hesitation. It's thirty thousand dollars for one night. Thirty. Thousand. Dollars. You've never made that in one night alone. Plus, he's young, hot, and a billionaire. Aren't you dying to see what he's like in bed? It's been a hot minute since you've slept with someone that young."

I sighed. "I know, and there is something about him that intrigues me, but also scares me." I took a sip of my coffee.

"You'll have your gun. If he tries anything unwarranted, shoot him in the balls." She smiled. "Plus, you've taken plenty of self-defense courses. I don't think you have anything to be worried about. He's just a billionaire who's bored."

"Maybe you're right. But I've never revealed myself to any of my clients. It's too risky. I have Stella to think about."

"Like I said, he already saw you. So there's nothing to reveal. Consider it a date as Brielle Winters, not Emmy Pine. Take his money, run, and don't look back. You are in control and you decide whether or not you want to see him again. That's if he even wanted to book you for a second time."

I furrowed my brows at her.

"I guess you're right. He already knows what I look like."

"THIRTY. THOUSAND. DOLLARS." She leaned across the table. "One night. That's it."

As we were talking and I was cleaning up the kitchen, my business phone dinged and there was a text message from Caden.

"Have you decided yet?"

"Yes. I'll come as my natural self for thirty thousand like you offered."

"Excellent. I want you to go to Bergdorf's this afternoon and meet with a woman named Lila. She has some dresses for you to choose from for tonight. Dresses that I handpicked. She's expecting you."

"I have dresses at home I can choose from."

"Like I said, she's expecting you. I'll meet you at the Chatwal Hotel promptly at six thirty. The penthouse suite is on the top floor, P2."

"I'll be there, Mr. Chamberlain."

"Looking forward to it. Again, it's Caden."

8

Brielle

After taking Stella to the park for a couple of hours, I dropped her off with my mom and headed to Bergdorf's. When I arrived, I asked for Lila. After waiting a few moments, a tall, lanky, dark-haired woman approached me.

"You must be Emmy." She smiled as she held out her perfectly manicured hand. "I'm Lila."

"It's nice to meet you, Lila."

"You as well. Follow me and I'll take you over to the fitting room where your dresses are hanging."

When I walked into the fitting room, I saw three dresses hanging on the hooks. One was red, one black, and the other a champagne color.

"Mr. Chamberlain specifically picked these three out for you. Try on whichever one you want first and we'll go from there." She smiled. "I'll be right out there waiting."

I rolled my eyes as she left the room and stripped out of my clothes. The first dress I tried on was the red one. It was an off the shoulder mermaid gown by designer Zac Posen. Before I slipped into it, I glanced at the price tag: $4,990. Good lord. I'd never worn a dress this expensive. I put it on and walked out of the room to show Lila.

"Beautiful. Simply beautiful. What do you think?" she asked.

"I like it. It's a perfect fit."

"I like it too. If you didn't notice, it also has an extended back train. Go try on another one."

The second dress I tried was a champagne-colored, Samar-beaded glitter tulle gown with a plunging neckline by designer Jenny Packman. This dress was a little cheaper priced at $3,990. I walked out of the room and stepped in front of the three-way mirror.

"That's lovely, but I feel the red dress was more you," Lila spoke.

"That's exactly what I was thinking. I'll go try on the last one."

I pulled the embroidered-tulle, V-neck mermaid gown by designer Monique Lhuillier from the hanger and slipped into it. This was the one. I stepped in front of the three-way mirror and Lila walked over to me.

"Oh my. Simply gorgeous," she spoke. "What do you think?"

"I think this is perfect for the evening."

"I agree." She grinned. "Go change into your clothes and we'll head over to the shoe department. I have the most perfect Jimmy Choo shoes that will be stunning with that dress."

After changing and trying on the Jimmy Choo stiletto black heels with the peep toe, she placed the dress in a garment bag, the box of shoes in a department store bag and handed them to me.

"Have a wonderful evening. You're a very lucky woman to be in the presence of Caden Chamberlain." She smiled.

I forced a smile and thanked her.

"By the way, should I return these tomorrow?"

"No. No, darling. They're yours to keep. Mr. Chamberlain purchased those for you."

"Oh. Okay. Thank you."

I texted Ben and told him I was done and, on my way out of the store. When I walked out the large glass doors, he was standing there waiting for me.

"Looks like you did well," he said as he grabbed my bags.

"That's ten thousand dollars' worth of stuff you're holding." I smiled. "Apparently, Mr. Chamberlain wants me to stand out amongst all the other women tonight."

"Considering what he's paying you, you should." He smirked as he opened the car door for me.

Caden

I tucked in my shirt, put on my cufflinks, dabbed on some of my Armani cologne, and put on my black tuxedo coat. Standing in front of the mirror, I made sure my bowtie was straight. Walking over to the safe in my closet, I opened it, removed thirty thousand dollars in cash, and tucked it into my bag. Heading down to the lobby, I climbed in the back of my limo and had my driver, Charles, take me to the Chatwal Hotel. When I arrived, I was promptly greeted by the concierge and handed my keycard. Stepping inside the suite, I set my bag in the bedroom and then walked over to the bar, where a bottle of bourbon was waiting for me.

Finally. I had waited for this night all week. My desire to fuck Emmy Pine grew deeper every day. It was all I thought about and it was all I wanted. One night with her was all I needed. I wasn't a patient person and the anticipation of discovering what was underneath her clothes was killing me. I called down to the bar and had them bring up a gin martini, neat with a twist of lemon. She'd be here in a few minutes and I was sure she'd want a drink before heading down to the event.

Brielle

I climbed into the car and took in a deep breath. This reminded me of the first time I saw a client. I grew out of my nervousness over the years because I was always in control. But somehow, I didn't feel in control of tonight and I wasn't sure why.

Ben pulled up to the Chatwal Hotel, opened the door for me, and helped me out.

"You look beautiful, Brielle. Have fun tonight."

"Thanks, Ben. I'll try."

"If you need me, just call. I can be here in a flash."

"I will, but I don't think it'll be necessary."

I walked through the opened door of the hotel, where I was greeted by the doorman with a nod and a smile.

"Good evening, Miss. I hope you enjoy your stay."

"Thank you. I'm sure I will."

"May I help you?" A tall man with a cheery smile approached me.

"I'm meeting Mr. Chamberlain in his suite."

"Very good. Just take the elevator up to the top floor."

I gave him a smile and he pushed the button to the elevator for me. Once the doors opened, I stepped inside and nervously took it up to the top floor. Once I approached his room, I lightly knocked on the door. When it opened, Caden handsomely stood there, his eyes raking over me as the corners of his mouth curved upwards.

"You look absolutely stunning," he spoke as he held out his hand.

"Thank you." I placed my hand in his and stepped inside. "This is really nice." I looked around. "I'm going to place my bag in the bedroom."

"Of course," he spoke.

After setting my bag down, I walked out into the living area, where he was waiting for me with a glass in his hand.

"I had the bar make this for you." He smiled as he handed it to me. "Just how you like it."

"I appreciate that. Thank you."

This was definitely a change for me. I was always the one offering my clients drinks. Not the other way around. I took a sip to try and ease the nervousness that was inside me. A nervousness that shouldn't have been there.

"Your eyes are blue. An incredibly beautiful shade of blue. Don't get me wrong, they were beautiful green, but I think blue suits you best. By the way, I was secretly hoping you'd pick that dress. It looks beautiful on you."

"Thank you, Caden. And thanks for the dress and the shoes."

"You're welcome. I have a question for you. Do you tell people what you do for work? I'm suspecting you don't, considering you disguise yourself."

"As far as anyone outside my very small circle is concerned, I'm a freelance marketing consultant."

"Excellent. So if anyone asks, we met through my company. If you're ready, we should head downstairs." He held out his arm.

I hooked my arm around his and we went to the ballroom where the event was being held. It was a fundraising event for a new wing at Mount Sinai Hospital. When we walked in, all eyes turned to us as if we were royalty. Men smiled and nodded at Caden as the women stared me up and down.

9

Brielle

"Caden, how are you?" A man approached, and I froze.

He was a client of mine that I hadn't seen in about a year. The nervousness in my belly intensified as I feared he would recognize me.

"Jim. It's good to see you. I'm good. How about yourself?" They shook hands.

"I'm good. Couldn't be better, in fact. You heard that Dee and I divorced?"

"I did, and I'm sorry."

"Don't be. That money-sucking bitch was worth every penny I paid her to get out of my life." He smiled. "And who is this beautiful woman on your arm?"

"Hi." I smiled as I held out my hand. "I'm Delilah Winters and I'm a marketing consultant for Mr. Chamberlain's company."

"It's a pleasure to meet you, Delilah."

When I gave my fake name, Caden glanced over at me with a narrowed eye.

"If you'll excuse us, Jim, we're going to go find some drinks," Caden spoke as he patted his shoulder.

"Of course. We'll talk later."

"What was with the fake name?" he asked.

"He's a client of mine. Except I haven't seen him in a about a year."

"And he didn't recognize you. So is Delilah your real name, then? Because I know damn well Emmy Pine isn't."

"And how do you know that?"

"Someone who disguises themselves for their job goes to great lengths to protect their identity and they wouldn't be foolish enough to use their real name."

"You're very observant, Mr. Chamberlain. Why are we here? Does your company donate to the local hospitals?"

"My father is on the board at Mount Sinai, and since he's in Europe, I step in when needed."

"Why is he in Europe?"

"He oversees our offices there while I tend to business here in the states."

"I see. So you run that big multi-billion-dollar company all by yourself?" I smiled.

"I have an excellent staff that helps. My brother was supposed to be in charge, but since he decided to leave the company and open his own restaurant, I was next in line."

"Why would he leave the company?"

"Because his passion is food. My passion is being in charge and running a multi-billion-dollar company. Just like your passion is providing sex to strangers for money."

"Believe me, it is not my passion. I do it for the money. And not every man that hires me wants sex. Sometimes all they want is to go to dinner and talk."

"Foolish men, as far as I'm concerned. There would be no way I could just take you to dinner and talk." He smirked.

"No. You're just foolish for paying thirty thousand dollars for one night with me," I spoke with an arch in my brow.

"Touché, Emmy."

We had dinner, mingled with some guests, and then it was time to go back to the suite. Over the course of the night, I only saw three people who were clients of mine. One that I was just with two weeks ago. He was with his wife and I couldn't help but feel sorry for her. If she only knew what her husband was up to in the afternoon when he was supposed to be at the office.

Caden and I stepped into the suite and I set my purse down on the table in the entranceway. He pushed a button on the wall and the curtains began to slowly close throughout the room. Walking over to me, he ran his finger down my cleavage.

"I know you're probably used to being in control, but tonight, I'm in control. Understand?"

"If you say so. It's your money." I smiled.

He leaned in and softly brushed his lips against mine as his hand slipped inside my dress and he cupped my bare breast.

"I will be the best you've ever had. That I can promise you," he softly spoke.

After our lips tangled for a moment, he broke our kiss, unzipped my dress, and watched as it fell to the ground. He took a step back and studied every inch of my body.

"Turn around," he commanded.

I stepped out of my dress and did as he asked, standing there in my black heels and black string panties embellished with rhinestones. I heard the intake of his sharp breath.

10

Caden

My cock hardened at a rapid speed. She was perfect. Her hourglass shape was to die for with abs that were tightly toned and visible. Her ass was tight and round. Not too small and not too big. I turned her around and stared at her natural C cup breasts that were perky with taut nipples that were begging to be plucked. My eyes made their way down to her pussy as my fingers delicately made their way up her inner thigh until they reached her slick opening. She was already soaking wet and I'd barely touched her.

I pulled away, took a step back, and told her to go into the bedroom and sit on the edge of the bed. As I watched her walk away in just her black heels and sexy panties, I took off my jacket and bowtie, unbuttoned my shirt, and threw it on the floor before making it into the bedroom. She sat there on the bed in front of me, feet planted on the ground as I took off the rest of my clothes. The only thing I could think about at the moment was her beautiful lips wrapped around my hard cock. I stood in front of her as the corners of her mouth curved upwards. I didn't even have to tell her what to do as she wrapped her fingers around me, and with a firm grip, gave my cock a few tugs. Her tongue lightly swept across me and I gasped, almost losing my breath when she took me completely in her mouth. My god, I had never felt so good. As astounding as her mouth felt, I needed to stop her because I was about to lose all control.

I pulled away from her and she looked up at me with those incredible blue eyes.

"That was fantastic, but I told you I was in control tonight," I spoke as I got down on my knees in front of her.

"Then by all means, take control." She smirked and I nearly lost it.

My hands fondled her breasts as she lay back on the bed while my tongue swept up her inner thigh. She let out a pleasurable moan as my mouth devoured her. With each flick of my tongue, her sounds became louder. I took my time and explored every inch of her. She was delectable and tasted sweet, just like I fantasized she would. Different positions soared through my head. Little did she know this wasn't going to be the only time we'd have sex. I was going to fuck her until she couldn't walk. I would make sure I got my thirty-thousand-dollars' worth.

As soon as an orgasm tore through her, I stood up and stared down at her.

"Are you on birth control?" I asked.

"Yes. Why?"

"I know you're clean because, in your line of work, I'm sure you get tested frequently."

"I am clean, and I do get tested, but I don't ever let a man not use a condom, if that's what you're saying."

"I'm clean too and I have the doctor's report to prove it in my bag. I always use a condom, but with you, I don't want to. I'm paying for this and I want to feel you naturally with no barrier between us."

Brielle

His voice was more commanding than simply asking. If the men I was with refused to use a condom, then I walked. It clearly stated in the terms of agreement that a condom must be used. Caden knew that. He read it, and yet, he stood in front of me demanding not to use one. I believed him about being clean. A man like him would never compromise his sexual health. But then again, he did hire an escort for the night. He trusted that I was clean, and somehow, I found myself trusting him.

"Okay. No condom," I softly spoke.

The corners of his mouth curved up into a smile as he hovered over me. Not once during our conversation did he lose his erection. I was impressed. Dipping his finger inside me, I gasped for air as he explored me. Not only was his mouth magnificent, his fingers were magical.

"You're ready for me," he whispered as he brushed his lips against mine.

With one thrust, he was buried deep inside me and my entire body trembled. Our lips locked while he slowly moved in and out. His tongue slid over my throat and across my neck as the warmth of his breath paralyzed me. My heart raced and my skin began to sweat. He picked up the pace for a moment and then rolled me on top of him. Our eyes locked as my hands planted themselves firmly on his muscular chest and my hips moved back and forth. His hands latched on to my breasts as he fondled them, tugging at my hardened peaks. Another orgasm was coming, and I couldn't control myself.

"Fuck, Emmy. Oh my God," he loudly voiced. "Come for me. Come right now."

I let out a soft scream as a roaring orgasm tore through my body. I was out of breath as I collapsed on top of him. He rolled me on my back and our lips collided. He thrust in and out of me like a wild beast, unable to be tamed. It was hot. He was hot and I found myself not wanting him to stop. He halted, let out a long moan and exploded inside me. He rolled off me and lay on his back, placing his hand over his heart while he tried to regain his breath. I rolled on my side and placed my hand on his. He turned his head and looked at me.

"I think you may have given me a heart attack." He smirked.

I let out a laugh.

"I've never had a client die on me, so please, don't do that."

"There's a bottle of champagne chilling. Would you like some?"

"Sure." I smiled.

He climbed out of bed, pulled on his underwear, and left the room. I lay there, taking in a deep breath as my body was still on a high. More often than not, I had to fake orgasms with my clients, but not with him. With him, they came naturally and very quickly.

"So tell me how you got into escorting," he said as he handed me a glass of champagne.

"It's a long story. So I'll spare you all the boring details. My mother got sick with cancer and got fired from her job just as I was going off to college. Her medical bills were piling up and she needed me to take care of her. I was a waitress and I met a woman who was an escort but retiring. We talked, she took me under her wing, and sent her clients to me. The money is good and a little hard to give up. I live a good lifestyle."

"And now, with my thirty grand, you can live an even better life." He winked.

I let out a long yawn and then finished off my champagne.

"You're tired and so am I. We should get some sleep," he spoke as he took my glass and set it on the nightstand.

He lay down and held his arm out. I snuggled against him with my head on his chest.

"Don't be alarmed if you're woken up in a few hours with me inside you."

"Thanks for the heads up." I laughed.

His arm tightened around me as I closed my eyes and prayed that he kept true to his word.

11

Caden

She was incredible and worth every penny like I knew she would be. I fucked her again and hard before the sun rose. I lay there, one arm wrapped around her and the other behind my head, thinking and struggling with the fact that this woman satisfied me more than any other woman ever had. It had been years since I felt like this and it caused me a great deal of anxiety.

I looked down at her and she opened her eyes. She stirred out of my arms and lifted her head off my chest.

"Good morning." She smiled. "What time is it?"

"It's eight o'clock. How about we order room service before we part ways?"

"Sure. That sounds good."

I reached over and pulled the room service menu from the nightstand as she sat up next to me and laid her head on my shoulder while we decided what to order.

"Eggs Benedict sounds good," she spoke.

"It does. I'll order us that and some fruit."

She climbed out of bed and went into the bathroom while I dialed room service. Suddenly, I heard the shower turn on, so I got out of bed and joined her. Might as well get one last fuck in before she left. I opened the glass shower door and stepped inside. She stared at me with a seductive look and took my rising cock in her hand.

"I was hoping you'd join me." She smiled as her lips tenderly brushed against mine.

"The thought of fucking you one last time was too tempting not to."

My hands fondled her breasts as my thumbs rubbed her hard nipples. She moaned as did I when she stroked my balls with her fingers.

"Get down on your knees and take me in your mouth, but don't make me come. I want to save that for when I'm buried inside you."

She got down on her knees and wrapped her lips around the tip, slowly making her way down until I was fully immersed in her mouth. I threw my head back as a moan rumbled in my chest. While the warm water beat down on us, she sucked my cock even better than last night, which I didn't think was possible. The feeling was euphoric as I placed my hands on each side of her head. She was too good at this and I couldn't hold back. The buildup was there and I was about to come.

"Oh my God!" I threw back my head and exploded in her mouth. "Fuck." I strained.

She stood up, looked at me, and wiped her lips with the back of her hand while staring into my eyes. I forcefully grabbed her and pulled her into me while our mouths smashed together, and our tongues made their way down each other's throat. Suddenly, I heard a knock at the door.

"Shit." I broke our kiss. "Room service."

I stepped out of the shower, wrapped a towel around my waist, and opened the door.

"Good morning, Mr. Chamberlain."

"Morning. Just set everything up over there." I pointed.

I walked back into the bathroom, finished drying off, and put on one of the hotel robes. Taking another out of the closet, I hung it on the hook next to the shower for her.

"You may want to hurry up before breakfast gets cold," I said.

She turned off the shower and opened the glass door.

"I'm done." She grinned.

I walked out to the living area, poured us each a cup of coffee from the carafe, and took the lids off the plates. When I looked up, I saw her emerge from the bedroom, wrapped in the white robe with her wet long blonde hair.

"I'm starving," she spoke.

"Me too. I think we both worked up quite an appetite. Do you shower with your other clients?"

"No. It's never been an option. With my wig, I can't."

"But with me it was?"

"I'm not in disguise, am I?" She smirked.

"No. You're not." I smiled.

"Tell me about you, Caden."

"You already know what I do and that's basically it."

"How is a super sexy thirty-year-old billionaire not taken?"

"Because it's the way I want it. How is a gorgeous twenty-seven-year-old not taken?"

"I have my reasons."

"As do I," I spoke. "Plus, I'm sure it's hard to be with someone doing the kind of work you do."

"I'd give it all up in a second if I found the right guy. But, unfortunately, the right guy doesn't exist in my eyes."

"Why is that?"

"He just doesn't. Anyway, I hope you felt you got your money's worth."

I narrowed my eye at her as I shoved a strawberry in my mouth.

"So far, your services have been exceptional. But I'll let you know for sure after I fuck you one last time. If you recall, I told you not to make me come in the shower."

"I can't help it you can't control yourself." She slyly smiled.

"Excuse me?"

She looked at me with fear in her eyes, but not actual fear, a playful fear. The moment I rose from my seat, she got up from hers, put her hands up, and started walking backwards.

"I said I can't help it if you can't control your cock." She bit down on her bottom lip.

"Oh, I can control it and I'm going to show you how much I can."

She ran to the other side of the suite as I chased her and she playfully screamed. Grabbing her from behind, I picked her up, carried her to the bedroom, and threw her on the bed. Untying my robe, I threw it on the floor and then ripped hers open, taking her nipples in between my teeth. Her laughter halted and turned into a steady moan. My cock was already hard again, so I spread her legs and thrust inside her, hard and deep.

"Tell me your real name," I spoke as I moved in and out of her.

"Why is it so important to you?"

"Because I want to know. You've already revealed your real self to me and I want a name to go with it. Your real name."

Her moans became louder and I knew she was about to come.

"Are you going to come for me?"

"Yes. Oh my God, yes! Don't stop. Please don't stop."

I halted.

"What the hell are you doing?"

"I want your name. No name, no orgasm."

I very slowly started to move again.

"Don't do this to me," she begged.

"Then tell me your name." I picked up the pace for one thrust and then halted.

"Oh my god, Caden."

"Do you want the orgasm or not?"

"Yes!" she shouted.

"Name."

"Brielle. It's Brielle. I swear that's my real name."

The corners of my mouth curved upwards as I rapidly fucked her and an orgasm tore through her body. The sensation overwhelmed me to the point that I had no choice but to come with her.

After we dressed, it was time to part ways. I reached into the safe in the room and took out the envelope with the money in it.

"It's all there," I said as I handed it to her.

"I believe you." She smiled.

I placed my hand on her cheek and softly stroked it.

"For the record, your services were beyond exceptional."

"Thank you. I'm happy that you're satisfied."

I leaned in one last time and kissed her lips.

"Goodbye, Brielle."

"Goodbye, Caden. It was nice spending the evening with you."

"I had a good time too," I spoke.

She grabbed her purse and her bag and walked out the door. I slowly closed my eyes as I clenched my fists.

12

Brielle

As I waited for the elevator, I stared at the door I had just walked out of.

"Get it together, Brielle. He's just another client," I spoke to myself.

Except he didn't feel like another client. I didn't know nor could I explain what I felt. The doors opened and I took the elevator down to the lobby, walked outside the hotel, and climbed into the car where Ben was waiting for me.

"How was last night?" he asked as he stared at me through the rearview mirror.

"Exceptional," I spoke.

"Wow. I never heard you say that before."

I just gave him a small smile and looked out the window as he drove me home. When I walked into my apartment, Stella ran over to me and gave me a big hug.

"Mommy! I'm so happy you're home."

"Me too, baby. Me too." I hugged her tight.

I spent the day with Stella and helped her with an art project for school. As I was cooking dinner and she was in her room coloring,

Sasha came over.

"Well, how was last night?" she asked.

"It was good."

"Good? Let me rephrase that. How was Mr. Chamberlain?"

"Sensational." I grinned.

"Oh my God." She grabbed my arm. "I knew he would be."

"Sasha, there are no words to describe him. His body, his hands, his mouth. I have never felt anything like it before. The way he made my body feel was unlike any other."

"Whoa, Brielle. Do you have the hots for him?"

"No. Of course not." I looked away from her and stirred the pasta sauce on the stove.

"Yes you do! I can tell. You're smitten."

"I told him my name. Not my last name, just my first."

"Oh wow. Seriously?"

"Yeah. Dumb, right?"

"I don't know. Maybe, maybe not."

"Listen, I'm going to take a break from the job for a while, so no more appointments."

"You have one tomorrow evening with Mr. Sanderson."

"Cancel it. Tell him I have the flu. I just made thirty grand in one night. I can afford to take a break."

"Sure. Okay." She looked at me strangely.

I was lying in bed, reading Stella a book, when I heard my work phone ding. Reaching over to the nightstand, I grabbed it and saw I had a text message from Caden.

"Can you come over to my penthouse tomorrow around seven o'clock. I need to discuss something with you."

"What do you want to discuss?"

"You'll find out when you get here. Can you come?"

"Yes. Text me your address and I'll see you at seven."

"I will compensate you for your time."

I couldn't help but smile.

"No need. Tomorrow evening is on me."

"Who are you texting?" Stella asked.

"Just a work client. I need to meet him tomorrow at seven so Grandma will have to watch you while I'm gone."

"Okay. Do you think she'll take me for ice cream?"

"I bet if you ask her really nice, she will." I tickled her.

The next morning, I took Stella to school and then headed to Starbucks to meet Sasha for coffee and a muffin.

"Hey, I'm running a few minutes behind. I'll be there soon."

"No worries. I just got here. I'll order your coffee."

"Thank you. See you in a few."

I shoved my phone in my purse, and before I could grab the door, it opened.

"Hey." I smiled as Caden stood there.

"Hey yourself. I was just on my way out."

"And I'm on my way in. I'm meeting my friend Sasha."

"Well, enjoy your coffee. I have to run. I'm late for a meeting. I'll see you tonight." He smiled.

"Have a good day. See you tonight."

I walked into Starbucks with my heart beating a mile a minute and fluttering in my belly. I took in a deep breath as I stood in the long line.

"Hey, did I just see Caden Chamberlain walking down the street?" Sasha asked as she walked up behind me.

"Yeah. He was leaving as I was walking in."

"Fuck, Brielle. He is more gorgeous in person. I had a total ovary explosion on the sidewalk."

I let out a laugh.

"I need to talk to you about him."

"What's going on?"

"He texted me last night and asked me to come over to his penthouse tonight because there's something he wants to discuss with me."

"What would he want to discuss?"

"I don't know and I'm really nervous about it."

"And you have no idea at all what it could be about?"

"No. I have no clue."

"Well, I guess you'll just have to wait and find out. Don't stress over it. I can tell you're stressing. That vein in your forehead is popping out." She pointed.

After we finished our coffee, I ran some errands and headed home. I spent the day cleaning until it was time to pick up Stella from school.

"Excuse me, Miss Winters?" Mrs. Pierce, Stella's teacher spoke.

"Hi, Mrs. Pierce."

"Do you have a moment to come into the classroom and talk?"

"Sure." I looked down at Stella and whispered, "What did you do?"

"Nothing," she whispered back.

Mrs. Pierce had her aide take Stella into the art room so we could talk in private.

"Is everything okay?" I asked her as I took a seat.

"Stella is a very bright child, like extremely bright. We've been testing her the past couple of months. Little bits here and there. Has she ever complained to you that she's bored in school?"

"Yeah. All the time. But aren't kids usually bored in school? I know I was."

"In Stella's case, she's bored because she already knows what the other children don't. She's reading at an extremely high level already. But I know you know that. Stella told me that you told her to pretend she didn't know anything and to learn with the other children."

"I want Stella to live a normal life, Mrs. Pierce."

"Life for Stella will never be normal with her I.Q."

"And how do you know what her I.Q. is?"

"We tested her."

"Without my permission?" I cocked my head.

"You actually signed the paper." She handed it to me.

I stared at my written signature that resembled my mother's handwriting.

"And what is her I.Q.?"

"Her test came back with a score of 150. Stella is highly intelligent and considered on the cusp of a genius level. I'm sorry to say that keeping her in this school is only stifling her intellectual abilities. She's too bored here."

"So what are you suggesting?"

"We're suggesting that you put Stella in a school for gifted children. Children who are smart like her. Have you heard of the Speyer School?"

"I'm sorry, but I haven't."

"It's a school for gifted and talented children, kindergarten through eighth grade. I've placed a call to them and they want you to fill out an application and set up an appointment to have Stella come in."

"If you think it's best for her."

"I do, but I will warn you that it's not cheap to send her there. The average tuition is around forty-nine thousand dollars a year, and with you being a single—"

"I can afford it, Mrs. Pierce. I make very good money with my job."

"I'm sorry. I didn't mean—"

"It's okay."

"Here's the phone number and address of the school." She handed me a piece of paper. "By the way, have you ever heard Stella play the piano?"

"No. We don't have one at home and she's never mentioned it. Why?"

"She's been practicing in the music room and she's extremely talented. She's been practicing pieces by Mozart. I'm surprised she hasn't told you."

"You know kids." I smiled as I got up from my seat. "Thank you, Mrs. Pierce. I will take everything you have told me into consideration."

"You're welcome. I'm sorry, Miss Winters, as much as we love Stella, she doesn't belong here."

13

Caden

C I couldn't believe I saw her. I had done nothing but thought about her since yesterday. I had this burning desire for her, and I didn't know why. The thought that she would be with other men paralyzed me. I wanted her body all to myself. She was the perfect woman for me when I needed to be sexually fulfilled. An escort, no strings, no commitment, and no love. Only sex. I found myself becoming possessive of her, and come tonight, if she agreed to what I proposed, it would be a win/win for both of us. She'd agree. I wasn't worried. She couldn't turn me down. She wouldn't. She was a successful business woman and all successful people know a good business proposition when they're presented with one.

After I left the office, I picked up some Thai food for us and headed home. It was six forty-five and she'd be arriving in fifteen minutes. I went upstairs and changed into more comfortable clothing and then set the table. As I was pouring myself a drink, the lobby buzzed me.

"Yes, Carson?"

"There is a woman down here named Brielle to see you, sir."

"I was expecting her. Send her up."

I stood in front of the elevator and waited for it to come up. When the doors opened, she stood there, looking as sexy as ever.

"Thanks for coming."

"No problem," she spoke as she stepped into the foyer. "What did you want to discuss?"

"We can talk about that over dinner. I picked us up some Thai food. I hope you like Thai."

"I do." She smiled.

I led her into the dining room where the food was waiting for us. I pulled out the chair for her and then offered her a drink.

"Wine?" I asked.

"Sure. Chardonnay if you have any."

"Of course."

I set her wine glass in front of her and then took the seat across.

"So what's this all about, Caden?"

"I have a business proposition for you."

"What kind of business proposition?" Her eye slowly narrowed.

"I want you exclusively to myself. Just for sex, of course."

"Excuse me?" She cocked her head.

"I want to be your only client and I'm willing to pay you very well just to be that."

"So basically, you're saying you want to buy me."

"Well, sort of. Listen, Brielle, I enjoyed our night together. I have needs and to be honest, having sex with multiple women is getting boring. There's always some sort of complication with them."

"What kinds of complications are you referring to?"

"They get attached quickly, or they want more, and it gets ugly. I'm a very busy man and I don't have time for that in my life. I'm willing to pay you seventy-five thousand dollars a month for the next six months as a trial. If all goes well, maybe we can extend it, and you must be available whenever I call. You don't have to give me an answer right now. Take some time and think about it."

"You're serious, aren't you?"

"If I wasn't, you wouldn't be here. You'd get the money, dinners, maybe a Broadway play here and there, and a few trips out of the deal."

"And I would only be exclusive to you?"

"Yes. You would be prohibited to see any other clients for the next six months. Which I think is a good deal. Not only would you be getting paid to be with me, but you wouldn't have to deal with all those other men."

"Eighty-five thousand," she spoke. "Especially if there's travel involved."

I sat there, picked up my drink, and narrowed my eye at her.

"I think seventy-five thousand is more than a fair price, but I'll meet you half way. Eighty thousand."

"Money is nothing to you, is it?"

"Not really. I have way too much of it and I have to spend it somewhere. Might as well spend it on a beautiful woman who would meet my needs without any drama. It's a win/win for both of us."

"You have yourself a deal, Mr. Chamberlain." She smiled as she extended her hand across the table.

"Excellent. I will have a contract drawn up for both of us to sign."

"A contract?"

"Yes. Of course. This is a business arrangement."

"Okay, then. When would you like to start our business arrangement?"

"Now." I grinned as I got up from my chair, walked over to her, and took hold of her hand.

※

She climbed out of my bed and slipped back into her clothes. This deal was going to be perfect.

"I'll have the contract drawn up tomorrow, and as soon as you sign it, I'll write you a check. Then you'll receive a monthly check on the first of every month. It'll be for services rendered as a marketing consultant."

"Sounds good." She smiled as she sat on the edge of the bed and put on her shoes.

My phone rang, and when I picked it up, it was my brother calling.

"I have to take this. You can see yourself out. I'll be in touch," I spoke as I climbed out of bed and went into the kitchen.

"Hey, Kyle."

"Are you home?"

"Yeah. I'm here. Why?"

"I'm in the lobby. I need to talk to you."

"Sure. Come on up."

When I walked out of the kitchen, I saw her walking towards the elevator.

"Have a good night, Caden. Oh, by the way," she stopped, "since we're going to be doing this, let me give you my personal number. The one I gave you before was my business number, which I won't be needing for the next six months."

I pulled her up in my contacts, erased the number she gave me, and typed in the new one. Walking over to her, I brushed my lips against hers.

"Enjoy the rest of your evening," I spoke.

"You too." She smiled.

The elevator doors opened, and Kyle was standing there.

"Oh. I didn't know you had company," he said as he stepped out.

"Brielle, this is my brother Kyle. Kyle, this is Brielle. She was just leaving."

"It's nice to meet you, Brielle."

"You as well, Kyle." They shook hands.

She stepped into the elevator, and as soon as the doors shut, my brother glared at me.

"What?"

"Is that—"

"Yes. That's the escort I was telling you about. I offered her a business proposition and she accepted."

"What kind of business proposition?" he asked as he followed me into the living room.

"For the next six months, she's all mine. I will be her only client."

"And how much is that costing you?"

"It doesn't matter, bro. She's worth it and there won't be any complications."

"You've done some pretty dumb shit in your life, Caden, but I must say, this really takes the cake. I can't believe you're paying an escort for the next six months for sex."

"It's not just for sex. It's also for companionship. I do get lonely sometimes, you know."

"That's your choice. It doesn't have to be that way."

"Yes it does, and you know it. With Brielle, I don't have to worry about all the bullshit that comes with women wanting more. I'm in control of her and she's getting paid not to give me any hassles or fall in love with me. This is purely a business deal. She can continue living a good life and I get my needs met."

"I will say I can't wait to see how this plays out."

"It'll play out fine." I handed him a drink.

14

Brielle

"Hi, Mom," I spoke as I walked into my apartment.

"Hi, honey."

"Is Stella in bed?"

"Yeah, but I just put her down a little while ago. I don't think she's asleep yet."

I walked into Stella's room and she opened her eyes.

"Mommy," she whispered with a smile.

"Hey, baby."

I sat down on the edge of the bed and gave her a hug.

"How was your meeting?"

"It was very good." I smiled. "Now go to sleep. You have school tomorrow. I love you."

"I love you too."

I kissed her forehead and walked out of her room. Walking into the kitchen, I grabbed the bottle of wine and poured some in a glass.

"What did he want to discuss with you?" my mom asked.

I brought the glass up to my lips and took a sip.

"He wants me exclusively for six months."

"What?" Her brows furrowed. "What does that mean?"

"That I can't have appointments with other clients. Only him. And he's paying me eighty thousand dollars a month."

"You're kidding."

"No. I'm not."

"And you agreed to that?" she asked.

"I did, because if I'm only with him, then I'll have more time to spend with Stella. Plus, it's eighty thousand dollars a month and I'm going to have a big tuition bill to pay if she ends up going to the Speyer school."

"Do you trust this man?"

I stared at her for a moment as I finished off my wine.

"Yeah. I do trust him."

※

The next morning, after I dropped Stella off at school, I met Sasha for coffee and told her everything about my deal with Caden.

"I just can't believe this. He's a hot single billionaire who can have any woman he wants for free. If he was married, I could understand, I guess, but he's not."

"According to him, things with women get complicated and messy because they want more. He knows he's safe with me."

"So why is he such a relationship phobe?"

"I don't know. He just said he has his reasons."

While we were talking, my phone rang, and Caden was calling.

"Hello."

"It's Caden. I'm calling to let you know that our contract is ready. Are you available now to come to my office?"

"Sure. Text me the address and I'll be on my way."

"I'll see you soon."

I ended the call and waited for his text message to come through.

"I have to go. Caden needs me to come to his office. The contract is ready," I spoke to Sasha as I grabbed my purse.

"I guess maybe I'd better get used to you jumping when he calls." She smirked.

"I'll call you later." I smiled.

I walked out of the café and headed to the address that he texted me. When I walked into the building, I was immediately stopped by a security guard.

"May I help you, Miss?" he asked.

"I'm here to see Mr. Chamberlain."

"I'm sorry, but Mr. Chamberlain isn't available."

I gently smiled as I pulled up Caden's text message and held up my phone in front of the guard's face.

"His text message says otherwise."

"Just a moment." He picked up his phone on the desk. "Your name?"

"Brielle."

"Brielle what?"

Without even thinking, I spat out my last name.

"Winters."

"There's a Brielle Winters here to see Mr. Chamberlain," he spoke into the phone.

Shit.

"Take the elevator up to the top floor," he spoke.

"Thank you."

I stepped into the elevator and pushed the button for the seventh floor. When the doors opened, an older woman with short black stylish hair looked up at me from behind her desk.

"You must be Brielle. I'm Louise, Mr. Chamberlain's secretary." She smiled as she extended her hand.

"It's nice to meet you, Louise," I spoke as I placed my hand in hers.

"Follow me. Mr. Chamberlain is waiting for you in the conference room."

I followed her to the end of the hallway, where we entered the room through two large wooden doors.

"Brielle, come in," Caden spoke as he stood from his chair.

As I took the seat across from him, he poured me a glass of water and set it down in front of me.

"How are you today?" he asked.

"I'm good. How are you?"

"Better now that this contract is done and you're here signing it." He smirked.

I picked up the contract and carefully read it over.

"I must be available at any time of the day when you call?" I arched my brow at him.

"Yes."

"Can you be a little more specific?"

"Perhaps I need to fuck you in the middle of the day. You are to come when I call."

"You will at least give me some notice, right? Because I might be in the middle of doing something and can't get to you as quickly as you need me."

"And what would you be doing?"

I sat there and narrowed my eye at him.

"I do have a life, you know. I could be in the middle of grocery shopping or just shopping in general or I could be at the gun range practicing my shooting." I arched my brow at him as I pursed my lips.

"You won't need that gun of yours for the next six months. You're safe with me and you know that."

"Do I really, Caden?"

He leaned back in his chair and stared at me.

"Fine. I'll give you notice."

"If it's the middle of the day, I have a room at the Warwick Hotel that I use."

"Seriously? You have your own room there?"

"Yes. It was my way of keeping in control."

"I could just come by your place." He smirked.

"No. I don't have clients come to my place, ever."

"I can understand that, but I'm your only client and I already know the real you, Brielle Winters."

Shit.

"I said no, Caden. My place is off limits. If that's going to be an issue, then you can have your contract back and we'll call this whole thing off."

"What are you hiding, Miss Winters?" His eye steadily narrowed at me.

"I'm not hiding anything. My place is my home for living purposes only. Not for work."

"Okay. The Warwick Hotel it is then if warranted. Is everything else to your liking?"

"There's nothing in here about when I'm on my period," I spoke.

"I thought about that. How long does it usually last?"

"About three days."

"You said you were on birth control. I'm assuming you're on the pill, right?"

"Yes. I am."

"And you start the same time every month?"

"Yes."

"Then send me those dates and I'll know not to call you. Now, is everything else okay?"

"Everything else looks fine."

He picked up a pen and handed it to me.

I took it from him and pressed it down on the paper. I hesitated for a moment, set the pen down and looked at him.

"Are you sure about this?" I asked.

"The question isn't if I'm sure, Brielle. The question is, are you?"

I took in a deep breath, picked up the pen, and signed on the dotted line.

"It's done," I spoke as I turned the contract around and slid it to him.

He signed it, reached in his pocket, pulled out a check and slid it across to me. I picked it up and stared at it.

"Like I said, you'll receive your checks the first of every month."

He got up from his seat, walked over to me, and placed his finger under my chin.

"I have some time before my meeting, and I'd like to check out that hotel room of yours." He smirked.

"I'll have to change first."

"Why?" His brows furrowed.

"Because the hotel only knows me as Emmy Pine in disguise."

"How long is that going to take?"

"I noticed you had a bathroom down in the lobby. I just need to send a quick text and I can have my things here."

"Okay. But don't take too long."

I pulled out my phone and sent a text message to Ben.

I need my bag and I need you to bring it to this address. Then I'll need you to drive Mr. Chamberlain and me to the Warwick.

"On my way, Brielle. I'll be there in ten."

"My bag will be here in ten minutes. All I need is about another ten to get ready. Outside your building, there will be a black sedan parked. I'll text you when to come down."

"A black sedan? You drive a black sedan?"

"I don't. My driver does."

"You have a driver?" His brow raised.

"I do. His name is Ben and he's been driving me for about four years. He watches out for me."

"What else don't I know about you?"

"Nothing."

"I need to make a phone call. Text me when you're ready," he spoke before walking out of the conference room.

I took the elevator down to the lobby, where I saw Ben walk through the double doors.

"Your bag, Madame. But why do you need it?"

"Because he's insisting that we go to the Warwick. I can't very well show up like this."

"Understandable. I'll be waiting in the car."

I took the bag and went into the bathroom, where I quickly changed into my black dress, stiletto heels, and my wig. After popping in my colored contacts, I threw on my fake lashes and colored my lips a cherry red. After putting on my sunglasses, I casually walked out of the bathroom, out of the building, and climbed into the car.

"*I'm ready and waiting.*"

"*On my way down.*"

Ben stood outside with the door open and Caden slid in next to me.

"Caden, I'd like you to meet my driver, Ben. Ben, this is Caden Chamberlain."

"It's a pleasure to meet you, sir," Ben spoke.

"And you as well, Ben."

We arrived at the Warwick Hotel and walked up to the front desk.

"Ah, good afternoon, Emmy."

"Hello, Joseph. I'd like my room, please."

"Of course. I was just thinking that I haven't seen you in a while."

He glanced at Caden and gave him a smile.

"That's because she's been with me, and after today, she won't be needing the room anymore. Isn't that right, Emmy?"

"I don't know. That's something we will need to discuss in private."

"Here's your key." Joseph handed it to me.

"Thank you."

"As always, enjoy your stay at the Warwick."

I gave him a small smile before heading to the elevator. Once we got to the room, I opened the door and we stepped inside.

"So this is where it takes place," he spoke.

"Where what takes place?"

"Where you've fucked a lot of men."

"This is it," I spoke as I took off my heels.

"After we're done, you are to cancel the room. I don't ever want to come back here again, and you won't be needing it for the next six months. So it's a waste of money."

"Are you uncomfortable here?" I asked as I removed his suitcoat.

"A little bit. I don't like the idea of that bed being used with so many different men."

"You're the one who wanted to come here," I spoke as I unbuttoned his shirt.

"Because I was curious. Just so you know, we're not going to fuck on that bed. I'm going to nail you against the wall with your legs tightly wrapped around my waist," he said as he slipped off my dress.

15

Brielle

"I'm going to have my driver pick me up and take me back to the office. So you're free to do whatever you want," Caden said as he buttoned up his shirt.

"Are you sure?"

"Yes."

He sat down on the edge of the bed and put on his shoes while I slipped back into my dress.

"When we go down to the lobby, make sure you cancel the room."

"I get the feeling you don't trust me, Mr. Chamberlain."

He stood up from the bed, grabbed his watch from the table, and slipped it on his wrist.

"I trust you. I just don't want you wasting your money on something you won't be using for six months."

We went down to the lobby and Caden followed me to the front desk.

"Joseph." I smiled. "I will no longer be needing that room anymore."

"Of course, Emmy. I'll cancel it now." He glanced at Caden. "I will say that I'm going to miss seeing you around here."

"Thank you. I'll miss you too."

We walked out of the hotel and I saw Ben waving at me from down the street.

"I'll be in touch," Caden spoke as he lightly took hold of my hand.

"Looking forward to it." I smiled.

As I began to walk away, he called my name.

"Brielle."

I stopped and turned to him.

"No offense or anything, but I don't ever want to see that wig again."

The corners of my mouth curved up into a small smile as I turned away and climbed into the car.

※

I had Ben drive me to the piano store on West 57th Street. The moment we stepped inside, a tall gentleman with salt and pepper hair dressed in a black suit approached us.

"May I help you?"

"I'm looking for a baby grand piano to possibly purchase."

"For yourself?" he asked.

"It's actually for my six-year-old daughter."

"Lucky little girl. Follow me and I'll show you our newest addition."

After being in the store for two hours, I walked out with a receipt in my hand for a Steinway baby grand piano in white that was going to be delivered tomorrow afternoon at one o'clock. I couldn't wait for Stella to see it. As we were on our way to pick her up from school, I received an email from the Speyer school. They had looked over my application and wanted to meet with me and Stella tomorrow morning at nine a.m.

I had always known Stella was highly intelligent. She was sitting up at four months, walking at nine months and putting sentences together at the age of one. By the time she was three, she could write her name and other words perfectly. When she colored, she never colored out of the lines, and when she played with her toys, her imagination was vivid. The only thing I ever wanted for my daughter was for her to live a normal life, 'cause God knew that mine was far from it.

After I picked her up from school, I took her to dinner so I could discuss the Speyer school with her.

"Listen, Stella, you're going to be late for school tomorrow."

"Why, Mommy?"

"Me and you are going to visit a different school that you might be going to in the Fall."

"Why?"

"It's a school for smart kids like you, sweetie. I'm so sorry that I told you to pretend you didn't know things. It was wrong of me. In this school, you don't have to do that, and you'll be with other kids who know everything you do. It'll be a better place for you. A school where you'll be challenged and not bored."

"Okay." She grinned.

I put Stella to bed, changed into my nightshirt, and sat down on the couch with a glass of wine. I had just turned on *The Bachelorette* when my phone dinged with a text message from Caden.

"Lunch tomorrow. One p.m. My office."

Shit. I needed to think fast because my piano was being delivered at that time.

"I'm sorry, Caden, but I can't. I have a doctor's appointment tomorrow at one."

"Cancel it."

"Okay. I will. Then I can't get a refill on my birth control pills, which means you'll have to start using a condom."

"Oh. Keep the appointment. How long is it going to take?"

"I don't know. Sometimes I'm there for at least two hours."

"I have a dinner meeting tomorrow night. So let's plan for the next

night. We'll go out to dinner and then back to my place for the night. I can send my driver to pick you up around six thirty."

"That's okay. I'll have Ben drop me at the restaurant. He still needs his job."

"Fine. Meet me at Per Se at seven."

"I will."

"Enjoy the rest of your evening."

"You too, Caden."

***

The next morning, Stella and I headed to the Speyer school. We took a tour and then they interviewed Stella in a separate room by herself. I wasn't sure how I felt about that.

"So, Miss Winters, do you have the contact information for Stella's father?" Mrs. Patterson, the school's director, spoke.

"No. Stella doesn't know her father. He took off the night I told him I was pregnant, and I haven't seen or heard from him since."

"Oh. I see. Will tuition be a problem? We do require the entire year paid up front."

"No. It will not be a problem. May I ask why you assume that because I'm a single parent and a woman that I can't afford to send my child here?"

"I'm sorry if you took my asking the wrong way. That's not what I meant. We just like to make sure that our parents can afford it because we don't want any hardships to come down the line."

"And that's why you require a full years' tuition up front? Just in case some parents find they can't afford it down the line?"

"We have found in the past that some parents had to pull their children out mid-year because they couldn't afford it like they thought they could, and that's not fair to the child."

"Well, if you accept Stella, I will be paying the entire year up front in cash." I smiled.

Stella walked into the office and took the seat next to me.

"So, Stella," Mrs. Patterson smiled as she folded her hands on her desk, "what do you think of our school?"

"I like it. I like it a lot."

"Okay. We'll be in touch soon, Miss Winters."

"Thank you, Mrs. Patterson. I look forward to hearing from you."

After dropping Stella off at school, I headed home to wait for the delivery of the piano. I had the perfect corner for it. All I had to do was rearrange a couple of pieces of furniture and I was ready.

16

Caden

The moment I saw Brielle step out of the car in her tightly fitted black dress with her hair flowing over her shoulders, my cock started to spasm.

"Good evening," I spoke.

"Good evening." She smiled.

I opened the door to the restaurant and placed my hand on the small of her back as she stepped inside.

"Good evening, Mr. Chamberlain. Follow me and I'll take you to your table."

We followed the hostess, who led us to a private booth in the corner. When our waiter approached our table, I ordered us both a martini.

"How was your day?" I asked her.

"It was good. How was yours? You look a little tired."

"It was stressful and long, but nothing I can't handle. I had lunch with my brother today."

"Speaking of your brother, he seems like a nice guy."

"He is. He's my best friend. We tell each other everything."

"So he knows about our little arrangement?"

"Yes. He knows. The night he stopped by the penthouse, he told me that he was going to propose to his girlfriend, Mercedes. They've been together a couple of years and they just found out she's pregnant."

"So I guess he's nothing like you, then." A smirk crossed her lips.

"How do you mean?"

"You're so anti-relationship and he's getting married and starting a family."

"I suppose. He's always had a string of girlfriends over the years, but Mercedes is the longest he's been with a woman."

"And now she'll be a part of his life forever with a child."

"I hope it works out for them because those tiny humans have a way of ruining things and people's lives."

"No they don't." She laughed. "I take it you don't like tiny humans?"

"Let's just say I'm not a fan."

"Why is that?"

"They're annoying and they cost a lot of money. They're needy, clingy, and too much of a responsibility."

"Children are a part of life."

"Not my life."

The waiter set our drinks down and then proceeded to take our dinner order.

"What about you? Do you like those tiny humans?" I asked as I brought my glass up to my lips.

"Yes. I love children."

"Then there's something we don't have in common. Enough talk about kids. How did your doctor's appointment go yesterday?"

"It went fine."

"Good. So you're all set with the refills for your pills?"

"Yes, Caden. There's no need to worry. You aren't going to get any offspring from me." She smirked.

"Just making sure."

When we finished eating, we left the restaurant and climbed into my car.

"I have to leave early in the morning for a meeting, so you can just let yourself out when you get up," I said as I placed my hand on hers.

"I'll just leave when you do. It's fine."

My cock ached for her all night and I couldn't wait to get back to the penthouse. The moment we stepped into the elevator, I grabbed her arms, pinned her against the wall, and smashed my mouth against hers. The doors opened and we stepped out, our lips never leaving one another's. She kicked off her shoes in the foyer while I slid the straps of her dress down, letting it fall to the ground. In one swoop, she was in my arms and I carried her up to the bedroom. I laid her down on the bed, placed my fingers between the sides of her panties and her flesh, and pulled them down. Pulling her to the edge of the bed, I buried my mouth in her, tasting the sweetness that I desperately craved. Sounds of excitement escaped her lips as my tongue circled around her swollen clit.

"Come for me. Show me how much your body loves what I do to it."

She let out a loud moan as her body tightened and her hands gripped the sheets. The wetness that fell upon my lips was intoxicating. I stood up and stripped out of my clothes. As badly as I wanted my cock in her mouth, I wanted to be buried inside her more. I flipped her over, spread her legs, and thrust inside her slowly, inch by inch until I was in deep. The heat that greeted me was euphoric and made my toes curl. The more I fucked her, the more I needed it. She was like a drug to me and I was the drug addict who couldn't stop. Her moans intensified as I thrust in and out of her at a rapid pace. I was about to come, and I wasn't ready for this to end just yet, so I stopped. Turning her on her back, I hovered over her and took her breasts in my mouth, one at a time, while I dipped my finger inside her. Her back arched and she threw her head back while another orgasm tore through her body.

My cock thrust inside her again, for now it was my turn. Moving in and out, I felt the heat rise between our bodies. Sitting back, I pulled her up and her legs wrapped tightly around my waist. My tongue slid across the flesh of her neck as I swiftly moved in and out of her. Her lips stroked mine as the warmth of her breath near my ear and her nails digging into my back made me tremble. I was ready to come, and I wasn't holding back anymore. Halting, a groan rumbled in my chest as I strained to give her every last drop of me.

I looked into her eyes as our hearts pounded out of our chests and our erratic breaths tried to calm down. I softly stroked her hair with my hand.

"That was the perfect ending to a long, stressful day."

"I'm happy I could take your stress away." The corners of her mouth slightly curved upwards.

I pulled out of her and slipped into a pair of sweatpants.

"I'll go grab us a couple bottles of water," I spoke.

When I walked back into the bedroom, she wasn't there.

"Brielle?" I called as I walked back down the stairs.

"I'm in here."

I walked into my study and found her sitting at my piano.

"I didn't know you had a piano."

"That's because the last time you were here, I didn't give you a proper tour of the house."

"Do you play?"

"I do," I said as I sat down on the bench next to her. "My mother started teaching me when I was four. My brother plays as well. In fact, he has one in his restaurant that he plays for his customers on Friday nights. Besides sex, this is another stress reliever for me. It calms me down and clears my head."

"Can you play something for me?" she asked with a smile.

"I'll play a few notes and then we need to get to bed."

I placed my fingers on the piano keys and started to play.

"You're really good. Your mom was a great teacher."

"She was." I slightly smiled. "She passed away five years ago. Heart attack."

"I'm sorry, Caden." She placed her hand on mine.

"Thanks. My father married her best friend two years later. He would never admit it, but me and Kyle believe they were having an affair."

"Wouldn't surprise me," she spoke.

"Really?" I furrowed my brows at her for what she said.

"When you're in my line of work, it's all you see. Almost all of my clients are married. And the ones that aren't are usually gay and using me to try to prove they aren't. Men cheat to gain their power and self-esteem back. They feel neglected at home, their needs aren't being met, and they like the thrill of getting away with something."

"And you're saying that's why all of your clients cheat on their wives?"

"Basically. Right before I met you, I had a client who couldn't go through with it. He told me about the problems in his marriage and I gave him a few ideas on how to fix it."

"So he paid you and he got no sex?"

"Yes. But he appreciated my advice more."

"Maybe you should have been a therapist."

"I wanted to be. That's what I was going to NYU for until my mother got sick."

"So why haven't you done it yet? It's not like you were working 24/7."

"I don't know. I guess time just got away from me."

"It's never too late, you know," I said.

A smile crossed her lips as she leaned over and kissed me.

"I think we should go to bed and get some sleep," she said.

"Good idea." I let out a yawn.

17

TWO WEEKS LATER

Brielle

Now that Stella was out of school for the summer, the nights I spent at Caden's penthouse would be easier. She never knew I wasn't home all night and I'd make sure I was home before she woke up for school. There were a couple of times I almost didn't make it because Caden wanted a long morning sex session. But now, she'd be sleeping in, so I didn't have to worry as much.

I arrived home at eight a.m. and found my mother sitting at the table with a cup of coffee and scrolling on her phone.

"Morning, Mom."

"Good morning."

"How was Stella last night?" I asked as I poured myself a cup of coffee.

"She was missing you, Brielle. Now that she's out of school and you're spending more time with her, I think it's harder on her when you leave."

"She knows I have to work."

"She's a child, honey, and she's getting older."

I sighed as I brought the mug up to my lips.

"Are you ever going to tell him about her?"

"No. Why would I?" I asked as I sat down across from her. "He's just a client and he doesn't need to know about my personal life. Plus, he doesn't like kids."

"Is he really just another client?"

"Of course. Why would you even ask that?"

"Because I've noticed a change in you since you've started seeing him. You're happier than you used to be. Sasha's noticed it too."

"I'm happy because he's paying me eighty thousand dollars a month and I'm only having sex with one guy. A hot, young guy. It's a refreshing change."

"If you say so. But I still think you're starting to develop feelings for him."

"I am not, Mother. End of discussion," I said as I got up from the table.

"Mommy!" Stella excitedly spoke as she ran up and hugged my legs.

"Good morning, sunshine. Did you have fun with Grandma last night?"

"Yeah, but I missed you."

"I missed you too, sweetie." I kissed the top of her head. "We have the whole day to spend together. What do you want to do? We can do anything you want."

"I'll think about it and let you know. Can I have cereal for breakfast?"

"As long as you have some fruit with it." I patted her head.

Two Weeks Later

I opened my eyes when I heard the soft sound of music playing. Looking over at the clock, I saw it was three a.m. I rolled over to find the empty space next to me. Slipping my robe on, I walked downstairs and followed the sound to his study, where I found him sitting and softly playing the piano.

"Can't sleep?" I spoke as I sat down next to him.

"Not really. I'm sorry if I woke you."

"It's okay. I enjoy hearing you play." I smiled. "Is something bothering you?"

"Even if it was, I wouldn't talk to you about it. That's not what I pay you for."

Whoa, I had no idea where that came from.

"There's no reason why—"

"Drop it, Brielle. I pay you for sex and sex only," he spoke in an abrupt tone. "Not to be my fucking therapist."

"Okay. I apologize."

I got up from the bench, headed upstairs, slipped into my clothes, and grabbed my purse. As I was walking down the stairs, he was heading up them.

"Where do you think you're going?"

"Home. We had sex and now I'm leaving."

"It's the middle of the fucking night. Get back in bed." He pointed at me.

I stood there and narrowed my eye at him for a moment and then continued walking down the stairs. I pushed past him, and he grabbed my arm. Silence fell upon his lips for a moment until I turned and looked at him.

"Please don't go. I don't want to be alone tonight. If it were any other night, I would let you go, just not tonight."

"Why?"

"I won't discuss my reasons. Please, Brielle. Just stay."

I stared into his pleading eyes.

"Okay," I softly spoke.

He let go of my arm, took my bag from me, and we walked up the stairs and to the bedroom. Slipping back out of my clothes, I climbed into bed and rolled on my side facing away from him. He wrapped his arm around me without speaking a single word. I lay there, eyes wide open, wondering what the hell tonight meant to him.

I awoke the next morning, and when I opened my eyes, Caden was already gone. I sighed as I looked at the clock. It was already nine. After I got dressed, I stopped at the bagel shop and picked up some bagels on my way home, for I knew Stella would already be up.

"Hey, you're up. Perfect timing." I smiled as I stepped through the door, walked over to the couch, and kissed her head.

"Where were you?" she asked.

"I decided that this morning was going to be a bagel morning." I held up the brown bag. "So I had Grandma stop by while I ran out to get them."

"Bagels!" She grinned as she jumped up from the couch and sat down at the table.

Caden

"I tried calling you last night," my brother spoke as he pushed a glass of bourbon in front of me.

"I was with Brielle."

"I figured as much. How are things going with your arrangement?"

"Fine." I took a sip of my drink.

"Just fine? I can tell by the look on your face something is bothering you."

"We kind of got into an argument last night."

"About what?" he asked.

"I couldn't sleep, and she asked me if something was bothering me. I told her I wouldn't talk to her about it and that I only pay her for sex. She got offended and was going to leave at three a.m."

"I don't blame her. That was pretty much an insult, bro."

"It's the truth. Did you want me to lie to her? I pay her to spend a little time with me and to have sex, not to discuss things in my personal life." I finished off my drink. "That's not what this arrangement is about."

"I'll be honest with you, your arrangement sucks. You know what else I think?"

"What else do you think, big brother?"

"I think this is all a sham. The moment you met her, you felt something, and you paying her a hefty check every month is your excuse to be able to be with her without having to show any type of feelings or emotions at all. You treat everything like a business, bro."

"You're wrong, Kyle. Dead wrong. I think she's a beautiful and sexy woman and that's it."

"Still not buying it. I'm your brother. I know you better than anyone else in the world. This is something you don't do, Caden. You don't fucking pay for sex. You've had a string of women over the years and let them go as quickly as they walked into your life. The problem is you don't want to let Brielle go. You want her on your terms and your terms only. It's time to let go of the past and live the life you were meant to live."

"You're right. I'm paying her, so it's all on my terms. Thanks for the drink. I have to go. I have a multi-billion-dollar company to run. And as for living the life I was meant to live, I already am. This cold heart is my punishment."

I grabbed my suitcoat from the stool and headed out of the restaurant. He always thought he knew everything. Hell, maybe he did. But the demons inside me kept me in check, reminded me of what I'd done and made sure that I'd never make the same mistake again.

18

rielle

B It had been three days since I'd heard from Caden. It was unlike him not to call or text me. He usually either called or texted at least once a day, even just to say hi. I was kind of getting a little worried, and even though I shouldn't have been, I couldn't help it. The days I didn't hear from him, even if it was a simple text message, I found myself missing him. I knew this was only a job and he was my only my client, but the feelings I felt for him were becoming stronger every time we were together. The way he spoke to me that night had hurt me. But his words were of hurt and anger about something that had nothing to do with me. Something happened on that night and I needed to know what.

While I was cooking dinner, Stella was practicing the piano. I tried to hire her a teacher, but she told me no and that she was okay learning by herself. She played incredibly well for someone who had never had a lesson. Listening to her play reminded me of Caden, and every time I thought about him, the knots in my belly tightened. After Stella and I ate dinner, she took a bath and I put her to bed. As I was lying in bed reading a book, my phone dinged with a text message from Caden.

"*I'm leaving for a business trip on Thursday to Chicago and I need you to go with me. We'll be back on Saturday. Have your driver drop you off at my penthouse at nine a.m. sharp.*"

"That's in two days."

"*And? I'm giving you notice like you asked. I'll see you then.*"

My belly twisted as I typed my next message.

"You don't want to see me tomorrow?"

"*No. I'll see you on Thursday.*"

I didn't know if I should have responded to that or not. So I just left it. I dialed my mom.

"Hello."

"Hey, Mom. Caden just texted me and said he needs me to go to Chicago with him on Thursday and we'll be back Saturday."

"That's fine, but there's something I need to talk to you about."

"What is it?"

"I'll come by tomorrow morning around seven a.m. That'll give us enough time to talk before Stella wakes up."

"Yeah. Okay, Mom. I'll see you in the morning."

I ended the call and set my phone down on the nightstand. Her tone sounded off and now I was worried.

I got up early enough to get dressed and make some coffee before my mom came over. I had some leftover chocolate chips muffins from yesterday that I'd made, so I put them on a plate and set them in the center of the table.

"Good morning," my mom quietly spoke as she walked through the door.

"Hey, Mom. Good morning."

I poured her a cup of coffee and set it on the table.

"So what's going on?" I asked as I sat down.

"I met someone." She smiled.

"What? When?"

"Last week. I didn't want to say anything until I got to know him a little better."

I cocked my head at her in shock.

"Who is this guy and where did you meet him?"

"His name is Steven. He's fifty years old, and we met in the meat section at the grocery store."

I arched my brow as I took a sip of my coffee.

"I hope he's not married."

"His wife passed away a few years ago. We've been talking every day and met for coffee yesterday."

"Oh my God! You couldn't tell me this?"

"Like I said, I wanted to get to know him a little better first. You know my history with men. Anyway, I really like him."

"And what does this Steven do for work?"

"He's retired."

"At the age of fifty?" My brow raised.

"He used to work on Wall Street, made very smart investments, and now he doesn't need to work anymore."

"So what does he do with his time?"

"He golfs, travels, and is heavily involved in charity work."

"Does he have any children?" I asked.

"No. He and his wife could never have any. The reason I'm telling you this now is because he wants to spend more time with me, and with your schedule, it's hard because you never know when Caden is going to call you."

"He gives me notice, Mom. You know that."

"Not enough notice as far as I'm concerned."

"So what you're saying is you don't want to be responsible for Stella as much anymore?"

"That's not what I'm saying. I just think you need to have a backup because I have a life too."

Wow. I can't believe she just said that.

"I know you have a life, Mom, but you agreed to help me with Stella."

"And I have been for the past six years. I'm always there the second you need me. Now I want to live a life for me too."

"Okay. I'll see if Sasha can be available more."

"What about Ben? You know Stella loves him and he loves Stella. He isn't driving for you as much anymore, so maybe watching her could make up for it."

"And what do I do when I need him to drive me somewhere?"

"You're a smart girl, Brielle. You'll figure it out. You always have. I'm sorry, baby, but I really like him. Maybe when your six months is up, you should consider retiring. You've saved quite a little nest egg already, and with the money you're getting from Caden, you'll have more than enough to live on, plus you can use it to go back to school."

"I'm happy you have my life figured out for me, Mom," I snapped as I grabbed my coffee cup and got up from my seat.

"Don't you dare take that attitude with me, young lady. I have been here for you since you had that child. Did you think I was going to do this forever? Maybe you should look into hiring a nanny for Stella. It's not like you can't afford it."

"Mommy, Grandma, what's going on?" Stella said as she walked into the kitchen rubbing her eyes.

"Hey, good morning, sunshine." I smiled as I walked over to her. "Nothing is going on. Grandma came over for some coffee and we're just talking. I'm sorry if we woke you."

"It sounded like you were using your outdoor voices."

"Come here, baby," my mother spoke as she held her arm out to her. "Give Grandma a hug. I have to go. Think about what I said, Brielle."

I rolled my eyes as she walked out the door. Maybe she was right. Maybe I should hire a nanny for Stella. If I did, then that meant my mom wouldn't be watching her anymore and she wouldn't be getting paid.

I spent the day with Stella and explained to her that I had to go to Chicago for work for three days. She wasn't happy about that, which made me even more upset than I already was. The older she got, the more difficult it was for her not to have me here. I only wished I could tell her that everything I was doing was for her.

"Mommy, don't be sad," she spoke as she placed her hand on my cheek.

"I'm not sad, sunshine."

"Yes you are. I can tell. You know what we do when one of us is sad." She smiled.

"Not right now, baby. I don't really feel like it."

"It doesn't matter if you feel like it. It's something that has to be done."

She picked up the music remote on the table, pressed a button, and "Hakuna Matata" began to play. Stella grabbed my hand and started singing. A smile crossed my lips as I got up and we sang and danced our troubles away.

19

Brielle

"Be good for Grandma." I smiled as I kissed and hugged Stella goodbye.

"I wish you didn't have to go," she pouted.

"You know Mommy has to work. I'm doing this for us, baby."

"Maybe you can find a different job. One where you don't have to leave so much."

My heart broke into pieces as I stared into her eyes.

"One day I will. I promise."

I grabbed my suitcase, said goodbye to my mom, and climbed into the car where Ben was waiting for me.

"It's getting harder on her," I spoke.

"She's getting older and she's more aware. She'll be fine. You're not the only working mother in the world. Plus, you're a single parent and you're doing a damn good job. Don't forget that."

I sighed as I stared out the window. I wasn't sure what to expect on this trip. Caden and I had barely spoken since that night. Ben pulled up to the hangar and my belly twisted in a knot when I saw Caden standing by his car. He walked over, opened the door, and held out his hand to me.

"Good morning," he spoke.

"Good morning." I placed my hand in his and climbed out of the car. My skin trembled, not only at his touch, but just by looking at him. It felt like it had been forever since I'd seen him.

He let go of my hand and I wished he wouldn't have. I followed him to the plane, and once we stepped inside, I took my seat while he went and spoke to the captain.

"We'll be taking off in a few minutes," he spoke as he sat in the seat across that faced mine.

"Okay." I looked out the window. With much hesitation and just a need for an answer, I asked, "So, how have you been?"

"Busy. Very busy," he replied as he pulled his laptop from his bag and opened it.

I expected him to ask me in return, but he didn't. His focus was whatever he was doing on his laptop. I turned my head and stared out the window as the plane headed down the runway. I thought about my mom and the conversation we'd had yesterday. She was right. She needed to live her own life. A life that didn't revolve around me or Stella. She deserved to be happy and to live the rest of her life with someone. She'd never trusted men, and the attempted relationships over the years that she found herself in never worked out because of her insecurities. I could relate. Once you were betrayed by a man, it was hard to ever trust again.

"You look like you're in deep thought. Is everything okay?" Caden asked.

"Yeah. Things are fine."

"Do you not want to be here?"

"Of course I do. It's just an issue I'm having with my mother."

"Do you want to talk about it?"

"No. Not really." I lightly smiled.

His eyes diverted back to his computer, so I pulled out my book and began reading. When the plane landed, we climbed into the back of a limo that took us to the Waldorf Astoria.

"Good afternoon, Mr. Chamberlain. Welcome back."

"Thank you, Edward." He smiled.

"Ma'am." Edward tipped his hat to me.

"Hello." My lips smiled.

He opened the door for us, and we walked into the grand lobby and over to the front desk.

"Ah, it's nice to see you again, Mr. Chamberlain." A bright-eyed blonde-haired woman smiled.

"Hello, Peyton. It's good to be back." He gave her a wink.

As she typed away at her computer, she kept glancing up at me. I immediately hooked my arm around Caden's and gave her a smile. He looked over at me in confusion.

"The key to the Presidential Suite," she spoke as she handed it to him.

I watched as she made sure her fingers lightly brushed up against his.

"Thank you, Peyton."

"If you need anything at all, give me a call," she seductively spoke.

I knew her type. She worked in this fancy hotel to try and sink her claws into the wealthy men that entered through the doors.

"If he needs anything, I will be taking care of him." I smirked as we walked away and headed to the elevator.

"What the hell was all that about?" he asked.

"Oh please. She was totally flirting with you."

"She always does when I come here. It doesn't mean anything to me."

"You don't find her attractive?" I asked as we stepped into the elevator.

"Of course I do. I think she's a very beautiful woman and I get the feeling she'd be exceptional in bed. By the way, do you do threesomes?" The corners of his mouth slyly curved upwards.

"I do. For an extra hundred grand." I raised my brow.

"I was kidding, Brielle," he spoke in a serious tone.

As soon as the doors opened, I gave him a smile as I stepped out.

"Seriously, I was joking. I know almost every man's dream is to have two or more women in bed with him, but it's not one of mine. I like to focus on one woman at a time."

"Good to know, Mr. Chamberlain."

"Come on. Tell me the truth," he said as he opened the door to the penthouse suite. "Have you ever done a threesome?"

"Why do you care?" I asked as I looked around the thirty-six-hundred-square-foot space. "But, if you want the truth, no, I never have. I've had men offer and I've turned them down, losing many clients because of it. It's not my thing either."

He grabbed my arm and pulled me into him, smashing his lips against mine, forcing them to part so his tongue could slip in between and greet mine. His hands roamed up and down my body and I could already tell he was sexually starved.

My fingers unbuttoned his shirt as he slipped his between the straps of my sundress and slid them off my shoulders. I gasped as his tongue slid across my neck and his hands groped my breasts.

"I've missed your body," he whispered in my ear.

I gulped as the palm of his hand pressed against my belly and slipped down the front of my panties. His fingers circled around me until one of them found its way inside.

"You're already soaked, and I need to taste your sweetness."

He got down on his knees, took down my panties, and began lightly stroking me with his tongue. My hands tangled through his hair as he pleasured me in the way I'd become addicted to. When I wasn't with him, I craved him. A craving so strong, I had to take care of myself while I thought about him. I'd never felt like that with a man before and it proved even more that when it came to him, my emotions ran way too deep. My body tightened as did my fingers in his hair as an orgasm rushed through me.

"Beautiful," he spoke as he stood up and placed my hand on the bulge that was hiding behind his pants.

"Here or in the bedroom?" I asked.

"Over here, on the couch," he replied as he took hold of my hand and led me there.

Before taking a seat, he took down his pants and then sat down, spreading his legs so I could kneel in between them. Taking his hard cock, I gave it a couple tugs before slipping it into my mouth. The moans that escaped him turned me on even more. With all the other men, I had to take my mind somewhere else, but with him, I wanted to be fully present and satisfy him in the best way possible.

"That's it. Oh God," he moaned. "Fuck, Brielle." He stopped me and brought me on top of him.

I slowly slid down his cock as I stared into his eyes, inch by inch until he was buried deep inside me. His fingers dug into the flesh of my ass while he took my nipples between his teeth. I moved back and forth and up and down, stroking his cock with the heat that resided inside me. Our moans became one as ecstasy filled our souls. Another orgasm overtook me as he let out a howl and exploded inside me.

20

Caden

I removed my hands from her hips and wrapped my arms around her back as she collapsed into me. Our breathing was ragged, and I could feel the pounding of her heart against my chest. She did most of the work and exceled in every way like she always did.

"When is your meeting?" she asked me.

"Tomorrow morning. I thought we could do some shopping today."

"Sounds good." She smiled.

I stared into her eyes and brought my hand up to her cheek. Flashbacks of that night filled my mind and startled me.

"What's wrong?"

"Nothing. We should get dressed if we're going out."

She climbed off me and I got up from the couch and headed into the bathroom. When I came out, she was already dressed and sitting out on the terrace of our room.

"It's beautiful out here," she spoke.

"Wait until you see it at night. Are you ready?"

We went down to the lobby and climbed into the limo that was waiting for us and had the driver drop us off a Bloomingdale's first.

"Are you shopping for anything in particular?" Brielle asked.

"Some new ties."

"And you can't buy new ties in New York, why?" She smirked.

"Because we're here in Chicago right now and we're shopping."

"If you say so. This one is nice. So is this one and this one."

"Not my style."

"I know. That's why I picked them. I think they would look great on you. Maybe it's time you step outside the box and wear something a little different."

"Excuse me? There is nothing wrong with the ties I wear."

"No. There's not. Not if you like boring. I'll be in the women's department." She walked away.

"I'll have you know my ties are not boring!"

I picked up the ties she showed me and took them up to the register. I'd show her. After I made my purchase, I headed to the women's department, where I found her trying on straw hats.

"Well?" She turned around. "What do you think?"

As much I wanted to tell her I didn't like it, I couldn't. The truth was she looked sexy as hell wearing it.

"It looks great on you." I smiled.

"Thanks." She grinned.

I had the driver drop us off at Eddie V's Prime Seafood and Steak. When we walked inside, people filled the space, waiting for their table.

"Welcome to Eddie V's. Can I help you?" A perky redhead smiled at me.

"How long is the wait for two?" I asked.

"Do you have a reservation?"

"No."

"The wait is a little over two and a half hours."

I reached into my pocket, pulled out a hundred-dollar bill and discreetly placed it in her hand.

"I'm sorry, how long did you say the wait was?" I winked at her.

"Let me check again." She flirtatiously smiled. "A table for two just opened up. Follow me."

"Impressive." Brielle smiled as we took our seats.

"Everyone has a price," I spoke with an arch in my brow.

"I suppose so." She picked up her glass of water.

Our waiter took our drink order while we glanced over the menu.

"Tell me more about your childhood," I said to her. "You're a very smart woman and I get the impression you were an exceptional student. I'm sure you never thought as a child that you'd become an escort for a living."

"You're right. I didn't. My mom was a single parent who worked two, sometimes three jobs to make ends meet. We lived in a shoebox with one bedroom. I never had much growing up, but I made do with what my mom could provide."

"What about your father?" I asked as I picked up my drink.

"I never knew my father. He took off when I was a year old. My mom came home from work one night and found all his things gone with a note on the bed saying that he couldn't do this anymore and he needed to start a new life somewhere else."

"I'm sorry."

"Don't be. I wouldn't have wanted a spineless coward of a man like that in my life anyway."

"Your mother never married, I assume?"

"No. After he left, she couldn't find it in herself to trust another man again. She dated on and off over the years, but the relationships never lasted very long. She always found a way to sabotage them out of fear. I always knew I wanted more out of life and was determined to get it. I was a straight A student, graduated as Valedictorian of my graduating class and received a fully paid scholarship to any college of my choice. But then, as you know, my mom got sick and I needed to give it all up."

I stared into her eyes as she told me her story. She was strong and brave, something I truly admired about her.

"Now that I've shared my story with you. It's only fair that you tell me yours."

"There really isn't much to tell. I grew up with a silver spoon in my mouth. I attended the most prestigious private schools and graduated from Columbia. My childhood was a good one. I have no complaints."

"Why did your mother teach you and your brother to play the piano?"

"She told us that nothing soothes the soul more than making beautiful music. I hated it at first. She'd make me sit for hours and practice. While all my friends were out playing ball and having fun, I was sitting behind a piano. But, truth be told, as the years passed by, I was grateful for everything she taught me. Playing relaxes me. In honor of her at her funeral, my brother and I played a song that was her favorite."

She reached over and placed her hand on top of mine while a beautiful smile crossed her lips.

"Okay. Enough talk about our pasts. Let's enjoy this delicious food sitting in front of us," I spoke.

※

The night was dark, and the rain fell in such masses that the wipers could barely keep the windshield clear. My voice grew louder, as did hers, trying to outdo the hammering sound that hit the windows. I was angry, so angry for what she'd done that I lost all control. The sound of the wheels screeching on the slick pavement hurt my ears, as did the screams that came from her. My eyes flew open and my heart pounded out of my chest when I heard Brielle calling my name while shaking me.

"Caden, wake up. You're having a bad dream. Caden."

I looked at her as the light of the moon sifted through the slit in the curtains and she stared at me. My body was encased with sweat and my breathing was constricted. I quickly sat up and turned on the lamp that sat on the nightstand.

"Are you okay?" she asked.

"I'm fine. It was just a dream. I'm sorry if I woke you. Go back to sleep."

"No. It wasn't just a dream. It was a full-blown nightmare. You were yelling."

I ran my hand over my face before climbing out of bed and going into the kitchen area for a bottle of water. I paced back and forth around the living room while I brought the bottle up to my lips. Fuck.

"Do you want to talk about it?" she asked as she stood in the doorway of the bedroom.

"What do you think?" I snapped. "It was just a nightmare. Go back to bed."

"Caden."

"I said go back to bed!" I shouted at her in a commanding tone.

Before I knew it, she was no longer standing in the doorway. I took a few moments to calm down and drank a half bottle of water. Walking into the bedroom, I sighed as I saw her lying there, turned the other way, as far away from me as she could possibly be. I climbed into bed and pulled the covers over me. She didn't move. I couldn't deal with her right now, for the nightmare I had wasn't a nightmare. I was re-living the events of that night. Something that I thought I'd buried years ago.

21

Brielle

I waited until he fell asleep and then I made my way into the other bedroom of the suite and slept there for the rest of the night. All I wanted to do was comfort him, but he made it very clear with his loud and commanding voice that he didn't want that. I got up at the crack of dawn, and when I tiptoed into the bedroom to grab some clothes to change into, I heard his voice.

"Where the hell were you?"

"I slept in the other room," I spoke as I rummaged through my suitcase.

"I pay you to sleep with me. Not in the other fucking room."

"Go back to sleep, Caden. Obviously, you need it." I stormed into the bathroom, shut and locked the door.

Once I pulled my hair back into a ponytail and changed into my clothes, I walked out of the bathroom and saw him sitting on the edge of the bed. I grabbed my shoes and walked into the living area.

"Where the hell do you think you're going?" he asked in an angered tone as he followed me.

"I'm going for coffee."

"I'll call room service and have them bring some up."

"No. I need some fresh air."

"Then go. I don't have time to deal with you anyway. I have a meeting I need to get ready for."

I grabbed my purse and shook my head at him before walking out the door. After I exited the lobby doors, I walked down the street and entered a Starbucks. Thankfully, there was only one person in line.

"Welcome to Starbucks. What can I make for you?" A bright and too cheery for this time of the morning barista grinned.

"I'll have a Grande americano with an extra shot of espresso."

"Name for the order?"

"Brielle."

"Is it okay if I just put 'Bri'?" she asked with an annoying grin.

"Sure. Bri is fine."

I stepped to the side and waited for my coffee. Once the barista yelled my name, I grabbed my cup from the counter and took a seat at a small table by the window. Whatever nightmare Caden had last night rattled him to his core and he was still feeling the effects of it this morning. But it didn't give him the right to speak to me the way he did. Caden Chamberlain had anger issues, and the more time I spent with him, the more evident it was.

I held the warm cup between my hands as I stared out the window and thought about my situation. I could break our contract and walk away. I was tempted. But then I thought about Stella and the money. Caden was right—he did pay me for sex—so what I needed to do was just give him that and stay out of his personal life. I could do that for the next five months, right? I needed to turn off my emotions and the feelings that resided inside me for him. He was nothing more than a job, and I was nothing more to him than the woman he paid to have sex with.

As I was finishing up my coffee, a text message from him came through on my phone. Sighing, I opened it.

"I'll be gone for a few hours, so I've gone ahead and booked you a massage, body treatment, and a facial. Your appointment is at eight thirty. I'll see you when I return."

Was that an apology? I didn't think so, but at that moment, I didn't care. A massage, body treatment, and facial were exactly what I needed right now. I checked the time and it was eight o'clock, so I headed back to the hotel.

※

I didn't think I'd ever been so relaxed my entire life. After my spa appointment, I headed back up to the suite. I wondered if Caden was back from his meeting yet with the hopes that he wasn't. I wanted to enjoy a few more minutes of pure bliss before the storm blew in. Opening the door, I looked around the suite and he wasn't there.

"Thank you," I whispered as I placed my praying hands together and looked up at the ceiling.

I went into the bathroom, put on some makeup, and fixed my hair. I had just changed into one of my maxi dresses when I heard the door open.

"How was your spa day?" he asked in a delightful tone.

"It was good. Very relaxing. Thank you."

"You're welcome." He walked over to where I stood and kissed my lips. "I'm going to go get changed. I would like to go to Navy Pier. I booked us a dinner cruise for later."

"Okay," I spoke as I looked at him in confusion.

I poured myself a glass of wine, took the cheese and fruit tray that was in the refrigerator, and took it out to the terrace. When I heard the shower turn on, I picked up my phone and called my mom.

"Hello."

"Hey, Mom."

"How's Chicago?" she asked.

"Eventful. Can I talk to Stella?"

"Of course. She's right here."

"Mommy!" Stella excitedly spoke.

"Hey, sunshine. How's it going with Grandma?"

"It's going good. I met her friend Steven last night. We all went out to dinner at Steak and Shake and then we went to Central Park. He's really funny."

"Wow. That's great. I can't wait to meet him." I sighed.

"When are you coming home? I miss you."

"I know, baby girl. I miss you too, and I'll be home sometime tomorrow."

I heard the shower turn off.

"I have to go, Stella. My clients are waiting for me. I love you."

"I love you too, Mommy."

I ended the call and took a sip of my wine. I wasn't sure how I felt about my mother bringing Steven around Stella so soon.

"Aren't you going to ask me how my meeting went?" Caden asked as he grabbed a piece of cheese from the tray.

"No."

"Why not?"

"Why would I? It's none of my business."

He sat down in the seat next to me, reached over, took the glass from my hand, and brought it up to his lips.

"Well, I'm going to tell you anyway. Chamberlain Essence came up with a new flavoring and I just sold it to the largest sparkling water manufacturer in the world. A multi-million-dollar deal." He smiled.

"Congratulations. Does that mean I'm getting a raise?"

"You're cute." He tapped my nose. "If you're ready, I'd like to head to Navy Pier now."

"Of course." I got up from my seat.

I swear this man was bi-polar. One minute he was yelling at me and the next he was as sweet as pie. I was going to take the sweet-as-pie version of him for as long as I could. As long as I kept my mouth shut, things would be fine.

22

Caden

We left the hotel and headed to Navy Pier. She was being unusually quiet, and I suspected it had to do with last night and this morning. I'd have to fix that. We walked past the carousel and I saw her staring at it.

"Do you want to go on it?" I asked.

"Why? Do you?" She smiled.

"I'll go if you go."

"Seriously? You, Caden Chamberlain, will go on a carousel?"

"Sure. Why not?"

I grabbed hold of her hand, purchased the tickets, and then we stood in line. When it was our turn, I asked her which horse she wanted to ride on.

"I like the pink one." She smiled.

She climbed on and I got on the brown one next to her. Once everyone was on, the ride started. I hadn't been on a carousel since I was a kid. I looked over at her, and when she looked at me, a bright smile crossed her face. As soon as the ride came to an end, I helped her off her horse, took her hand, and we explored Navy Pier before it was time for our dinner cruise.

"Did I mention that holding my hand costs extra?" She smirked.

"Is that so?" I arched my brow.

"Yep."

"Then tonight I shall pay you, not in cash, but in extra orgasms." I winked.

"Deal." She grinned.

After our dinner cruise, we headed back to the hotel and barely made it into the suite before I had her naked and pinned up against the wall, holding her arms above her head and taking her from behind. Beads of sweat formed on my head as I struggled to hold back. I pulled out, turned her around, and lifted her up as her legs securely wrapped around my waist. I thrust in and out while devouring her neck. An orgasm ripped through her, causing my cock to spasm and explode inside her. I carried her to the bedroom, still buried deep inside, and gently laid her on the bed.

The next morning, I opened my eyes and stared at her while she peacefully slept. Feelings deep inside me were rising to the surface, and as much as I hated to admit it, I was falling for this woman, but the demons inside me kept reminding me of my past. I was in my own personal hell and they wouldn't let me out. I didn't deserve to be let out.

"Good morning." She smiled as her eyes opened and she caught me staring at her. "Were you watching me sleep?"

"I was. You looked so peaceful. Did you sleep well?"

"I did. How about you?"

"Yes. It was a good night. We need to get ready, have breakfast, and get to the airport. My plane will be here in a couple of hours."

She reached up and kissed my lips before climbing out of bed. But before her feet hit the floor, I grabbed hold of her wrist. She turned and our eyes met. I didn't know why I did that. It was just a reaction.

"Is something wrong?" she asked.

"I—I was just wondering if you wanted room service or if you wanted to go down to the restaurant."

"I don't care. You pick." She grinned as she climbed out of bed.

I watched her as she walked her naked body to the bathroom. I craved her in every way possible and my cock was rising to the occasion. As soon as she started the shower, I climbed out of bed and joined her.

"I do believe I owe you another orgasm for you letting me hold your hand yesterday," I spoke as my hands ran down the front of her body.

After I made good on my word and pleasured her in the shower, I stepped out, wrapped the towel around my waist, and began shaving. As soon as she was finished, she slipped into her robe and stood at the sink next to me while she put on her makeup.

"Damn it," I said as I set down my shaver.

"You cut yourself," she spoke as she grabbed a tissue. "Here, let me." A smile crossed her lips. "You need to be more careful, Mr. Chamberlain. You don't want to scar up that sexy face of yours."

I placed my hand over hers, which was holding the tissue on my cut.

"I usually am very careful, but someone was distracting me."

"Then keep your eyes to yourself."

She removed the tissue and threw it in the wastebasket.

"Kind of hard to do when a sinfully sexy woman is standing right next to me." I smiled.

She returned my smile and brought her lips up to where I cut myself.

"All better."

※

After enjoying a delicious breakfast down at the hotel restaurant, we headed to the front desk to check out.

"Good morning, Mr. Chamberlain." Peyton flashed a wide smile.

"Good morning, Peyton. I'll be checking out."

"Did everything meet your needs?" she asked.

I glanced over at Brielle. "Yes, my needs were fully met."

She looked at me and swallowed hard.

"I hope you'll be visiting us again soon."

"Thank you, Peyton, and don't worry, WE will be back." Brielle smiled as she hooked her arm in mine.

As soon as we walked away, I glanced over at her.

"You're a very bad girl."

"I aim to please." She winked.

23

Caden

"I can drive you home," I spoke as we sat on the plane.

"No. It's fine. Ben is picking me up."

"But why? I said I can drive you home. I'd like to see where you live."

"Thank you, Caden, but Ben will already be there."

"We don't land for another hour. Call him and tell him that I'm taking you home."

"Next time." She smiled.

"I get the feeling you don't want me to know where you live."

"That's not true at all."

"Then call him right now and tell him that I'm taking you home. It's actually an order, Brielle. We're in this for the next five months and you've been to my place plenty of times. I want to see where you live."

I could see the hesitation all over her face and I didn't understand it. It wasn't like I was a stranger to her.

"Okay. I'll call him and let him know."

As soon as the plane landed, we climbed into the car and she gave my driver her address. As soon as he pulled up to the curb of the building, I climbed out first and helped her out.

"Impressive," I spoke as I looked up at the building.

"Thank you for a wonderful trip." She kissed my lips.

"I would like to come up and see your place."

"No, Caden." She sighed. "Listen, my place is a disaster right now and I'm going to spend the rest of the day cleaning it. I would be totally embarrassed if you saw it in the state it's in. Next time."

I narrowed my eye at her for a moment and, all of a sudden, a child ran into me.

"Sorry, mister," he said as he ran by.

"Damn kids. Where the hell are the parents? Nothing annoys me more than a parent that can't keep an eye on their monsters."

"I know, right?" she spoke.

"Go clean up your place. I need to get going." I leaned in and kissed her. "I'll be in touch."

Something wasn't sitting right with me. Her refusal to let me up to her apartment raised a lot of suspicion. Instead of going home, I went to Kyle's restaurant to talk to him.

"How was Chicago, bro?" He smiled as I walked into the kitchen.

"It was good. I closed the deal." I grinned.

"Awesome. More millions for you." He smirked. "Since you're here, make yourself useful. Chop up this garlic for me." He handed me a knife. "So how's Brielle doing?"

"She's the reason I'm here. Something is going on with her."

"How do you mean?"

"I had to practically force her to let me drive her home. For some reason, she didn't want me to know where she lives."

"She's a smart girl. But she should know that you can find that out on your own."

"When I finally told her she had no choice, she let me take her home but then wouldn't let me go up to see her place. We've known each other for weeks and we're going to be together for the next five months. I get the feeling she's hiding something."

"I think you're being a bit paranoid, Caden. Maybe she doesn't trust you. Can you chop that garlic a little finer, please?"

I shot him a look.

"Let me ask you this. Why is it so important to you that you see her place?" he asked.

"I don't know. I just want to see how she lives. She gave me the excuse that her place was a disaster and she'd be embarrassed if she let me up. And trust me, she's not a slob, so I'm not buying that story."

"Why do you want to see how she lives? All she is to you is sex. You pay her for sex and sex only. Unless—" His eye narrowed at me.

"Don't be an idiot," I said.

"You have feelings for her." He pointed his knife at me.

"No I don't."

"Yes. You do. For fuck sakes, bro, just admit it. This is me you're talking to."

"I think she's kind of cool and she's fun to hang out with."

"You think she's cool? Seriously?"

"Fine." I slammed down the knife I was holding. "She's an incredible woman, and when I'm not with her, I can't stop thinking about her. And when I am with her, I don't want it to end. But you and me both know that nothing can ever come of it."

"No. That's what you believe. Not what I believe. You've kept yourself locked up in a prison and threw away the key. What happened eight years ago is in the past. Are you really going to punish yourself for the rest of your life? Goddamn it, Caden, it was an accident. You deserve to be happy like everyone else in the world."

"I've been having nightmares about that night," I said. "That hasn't happened in years."

"Because you're falling in love with Brielle and it scares the fuck out of you. So you need to keep reminding yourself the reason why you locked up your heart and soul. If you still want to punish yourself then break the contract and get out of this stupid thing you have going on with her. But if you want to be happy, talk to her. Tell her what happened. Be real with her."

"I can't."

He let out a heavy sigh. "Listen, I'm looking for a couple art pieces for the restaurant. How about coming to the art gallery with me tomorrow? Mercedes is spending the day with her mom. We can make it a bro day. We haven't had that in a while."

"Sure. I'll go."

"Great. You can pick me up at noon." He smiled.

Later that evening, I was sitting on the couch with my laptop and I found myself thinking about Brielle, so I decided to send her a text message.

"Hi. What are you up to right now?"

"Hi. Having dinner with my mom and Sasha. What are you up to?"

"Not much. Just sitting on the couch doing some work. I was hoping I could see you."

"I'm sorry, but I'm busy."

"I understand."

"Is everything okay?"

"Everything's fine. Enjoy the rest of your evening."

"You too. If you want to talk, you can call me later."

I didn't respond. I wouldn't lie and say I wasn't disappointed, because I was. This growing need to be with her was getting out of control and it needed to be stopped.

24

Brielle

I sighed as I set my phone down.

"Was that Caden?" Sasha asked.

"Who's Caden, Mommy?" Stella asked.

I shot Sasha a look.

"He's one of my clients, sunshine. If you're finished eating, why don't you go and practice playing the piano."

"Okay." She smiled as she took her last bite of sweet and sour chicken.

"Caden wanted to see me tonight," I spoke to my mom and Sasha.

"You just spent almost three days with the man," Sasha said.

"Either he's a sex addict or he's falling for you," my mother spoke.

"He's not a sex addict. Well, he might be." I furrowed my brows. "And he's definitely not falling for me. I let him drive me home today," I blurted out.

"What?!" Sasha exclaimed. "Are you nuts?"

"He basically forced me to. He wanted to come up and see the apartment and I had to make up an excuse as to why I wouldn't let him."

"Brielle, you're going to have to tell him about Stella sooner or later."

"I can't, Mom. He hates kids."

"What kind of man hates children?" Sasha asked.

"A man like Caden Chamberlain, that's who. He doesn't ever want children or a family. It's really sad."

"You can't keep hiding Stella. Now that he knows your address, what's going to stop him from coming over here one night out of curiosity? I shouldn't have to tell you not to underestimate a man like him," Sasha said.

"Besides," my mother spoke, "he's your client and Stella has nothing to do with it. He can't hold that against you. It says nothing in your contract that you have to discuss your personal life with him. All you are is a business transaction."

"Thanks, Mom." I narrowed my eye at her.

"I'm sorry, sweetheart, but it's the truth. Stella is none of his business. And if he hates children the way you said he does, then I don't want her anywhere near him."

I sighed and pushed my plate away. Sasha was right. What if he came over unannounced? Then what? Keeping Stella a secret from him for the next five months wasn't going to be easy. Maybe he'd be okay with knowing I had a daughter. Maybe I was just overthinking it.

The next morning, I took Stella and Ben to breakfast and then I had him drive us around the city while I ran some errands.

"How would you like to go to the art gallery today?" I asked Stella. "A friend of mine has a couple pieces of her art on display and I'd like to go look at them."

"Sure, Mommy. I like to look at all the paintings."

Ben dropped us off at the art gallery on East 70th Street. I grabbed Stella's hand and when we walked inside, I saw my friend Amelia standing by her artwork.

"Brielle, Stella!" She hugged us both. "My gosh, you're growing up way too fast, little one." She smiled.

Amelia and I got to talking about her art and Stella asked if she could go over to the table and take a cookie.

"Sure. You can have one and then come right back."

"Okay."

꙳

Caden

"What do you think about this piece for the restaurant?" Kyle asked.

"It's nice. I think it would look good there."

"Excellent. I'm going to go get the associate and tell her that I want to purchase it."

"I'm going to walk around a bit," I spoke.

I was standing in front of a painting. An odd one at that. It was a portrait of a naked woman lying on the floor in a room with several cats staring down at her.

As I was studying it, I felt a tug on my pants. When I looked down, a tiny human with bright blue eyes stared up at me.

"Hi." She smiled.

"Excuse me, but do you know how expensive these pants are? I really don't need your greasy little fingers touching them."

"They're not greasy. Would you like a piece of my cookie?" She held it up.

"No. I do not want a piece of your cookie. Where are your parents?"

"My mom is talking to her friend. What do you think this painting is telling us?" she asked.

Was this kid serious?

"I haven't a clue. Can you please take your cookie elsewhere?"

"Stella, I told you—"

The moment I heard that voice, I turned around and stared at the woman a few feet away from me.

"Mommy, I was just looking at this painting."

Brielle cupped her hand over her mouth as a look of shock swept over her face.

"Mommy?" I said in an angry tone.

"I can explain."

"Do you know my mom?" the child asked.

"I do and now I wish I didn't."

I turned and walked the other way as fast as I could. I found Kyle up at the desk and told him that I'd be waiting for him in the car.

"Wait, Caden. What's wrong?"

I walked out of the gallery and paced back and forth on the sidewalk. Anger soared through me as I clenched my fists. I couldn't believe this. I couldn't believe she had a kid and didn't tell me.

"Caden, wait. Please. I can explain," Brielle pleaded as she stood on the sidewalk.

"Explain what? That you had a child you never mentioned?" I angrily spoke through gritted teeth. "I cannot believe you."

"Stella is my personal life. What we have is a business arrangement. I didn't think I had to tell you that I had a daughter. I keep both my professional life and my business life completely separate."

"Which brings me to another point. What kind of mother sells her body for money when she has a child?"

She raised her hand and I grabbed her wrist before she could slap me across the face.

"As of this moment, our contract is null and voided. I don't ever want to see you again. And to think I was developing feelings for you." I let go of her wrist and began walking to my limo.

"You're incapable of any feelings!" she shouted. "You're nothing but a mean, arrogant, and egotistical man who isn't capable of love."

I stood there for a moment, clenching my fist and taking in a deep breath.

"Caden, what's going on?" Kyle asked as he stepped out of the art gallery.

"Let's go, now!" I commanded as I climbed into the car.

25

Brielle

I stood there and watched his limo pull away from the curb. My body was shaking as tears started to fall down my face. I wiped my eyes, for I couldn't let Stella see me crying. I composed myself and walked back into the art gallery to fetch her.

"Is something wrong, Mommy?" she asked.

"No, sweetie. We need to go home now."

"Who was that man and why did he upset you?"

"He's a friend and he didn't upset me, sunshine. Come on, we have to go."

The moment we climbed into the car, Ben looked back at me to make sure I was okay.

"We're ready to go home now," I said.

"Sure thing, Brielle."

I pulled out my phone and sent a text message to my mom.

"*Caden found out about Stella and it didn't go well. Can I please drop her off with you for a while? I need to be alone.*"

"*Shit. Of course. Steven and I are heading back home now. Just take her home and I'll stop by and pick her up. I'll figure out some excuse.*"

"Thanks, Mom."

Trying to hold it together was nearly impossible when all I wanted to do was fall apart. But I couldn't. I wouldn't let Stella see me like that. When we arrived home, Stella went right over to the piano and started practicing while I went into the kitchen and cleaned up. A few moments later, there was a knock at the door, and when I opened it, Steven and my mom stood there. She could tell I was upset, but she didn't want to make a big deal about it in front of Stella.

"Grandma! Steven! What are you doing here?" she asked.

"Hello, my sweet girl. How would you like to spend the rest of the day and night with me and Steven? We have tickets to see *Annie* on Broadway!" she spoke with excitement.

"Really? Mommy, can I?" She jumped up and down.

"Yes. Of course you can." I smiled as I patted her head. "Why don't you go change your clothes?"

"Okay."

"And pack your pjs because we'll be home kind of late and you can sleep in your room at my house," my mom said.

"How did you get tickets to see *Annie* that fast?" I asked.

"Steven has connections." She smiled. "What happened?"

"We were at the art gallery and so was he. Of all the people she chose to talk to, she chose him. That's when he found out. He told me he never wanted to see me again and that our contract was over." Tears filled my eyes.

"Oh, Brielle." She placed her hands firmly on my shoulders. "It's best this way. You know that, right?"

I stood there and slowly nodded my head as I tried to stop the tears from falling.

"Okay, I'm ready!" Stella announced.

I knelt down and kissed her forehead.

"You be good for Grandma and Steven and I'll see you in the morning. Have fun watching *Annie*. I love you."

"I love you too, Mommy."

The moment they stepped out, I shut the door, leaned up against it, and slowly fell to the ground while the tears I had been holding back all that time flooded my eyes.

Caden

"Do you believe it? Do you believe she had a kid this whole time and didn't tell me?" I asked Kyle.

"Calm down, Caden."

"Don't tell me to calm down. I'm pissed as hell. I told her I never wanted to see her again and that our contract was over."

"A little harsh. Don't you think?"

"Harsh? Are you fucking kidding me? She lied to me!"

The car pulled up to my building and Kyle and I climbed out and went up to my penthouse. I walked over to the bar and poured us each a scotch.

"She didn't lie to you, bro. If you would have asked her if she had a kid and she said no, then she would have lied to you. But you never asked and she never told you. All she did was keep her kid out of this damn business arrangement you had."

"It doesn't matter. She should have told me." I downed my drink and poured another one.

"Why? Why should she have told you? Again, the two of you had a business deal. Do you know the personal lives of every single one of your clients?"

"That's different!" I snapped.

"No. No it's not. The only reason you're so pissed off right now is because you fell for her. If feelings weren't involved, you wouldn't give a damn. And don't you dare sit there and tell me that I'm wrong."

I didn't say a word as I downed my second drink and slammed it down on the bar.

"What kind of woman sells her body when she has a kid?" I shouted.

"The kind of woman where apparently no father is involved, and she needs to support her child. You don't know her story, man. She told you what she wanted you to know, just like you told her what you wanted her to know. You weren't completely honest with her about your past."

"Why the hell would I be?"

"Exactly. And why would she? Think about it. I have to go. Mercedes will be home soon. Call me later when you calm down and can think rationally." The moment he stepped inside the elevator and the doors shut, I picked up my glass and threw it against the wall.

26

Brielle

I lay on my bed with my head in Sasha's lap as she stroked my hair and the tears that wouldn't stop flowing fell down my face.

"I can't believe he reacted that way. You should have seen him. He was so angry."

"He had no right to be angry. You didn't do anything wrong."

"What am I going to do, Sasha?"

"You're going to pick yourself up and go on with your life."

"It hurts so much. I'm in love with him."

"I know you are, sweetie, and it sucks he's such an asshole. But you're Brielle fucking Winters and you don't let a man keep you down."

"I've never felt this way before. Not even when Daniel left. I've never been in love before until Caden."

"I don't know what to say, Bri. I'm sorry he did this to you, but that right there shows you what kind of man he is. He isn't good for you or for Stella. You need to forget about him and move on with your life."

"I'm done with escorting. Totally done. I can't do it anymore."

"And that's fine. You have money saved. You don't need to escort anymore. Take some time and think about what you want to do. Before you know it, Caden Chamberlain will be nothing but a distant memory."

After she left, I started the bath, poured some lavender scented bubbles in it, and climbed in, sinking all the way down until the water was up to my neck. The physical pain in my heart was unbearable, so unbearable that it hurt to breathe. My head was a mess and I needed to get a grip on things. Maybe I should take Stella and move out of New York. Start over, somewhere fresh. Maybe somewhere by the ocean.

I climbed out of the tub, dried myself off, and changed into my pajamas. Walking into the kitchen, I poured myself a glass of wine and took it, along with my laptop, to my bedroom. Pulling up a map of the U.S., I looked at all the states. Florida? Nah. South Carolina? Maybe. Vermont? Perhaps. If I left, I'd be leaving my family and friends and taking Stella away from her grandmother. I wasn't sure if she'd adjust. I sighed as I shut my laptop and set it to the side. Closing my eyes, I fell asleep.

The next day, my mom brought Stella home.

"Hey there, sunshine. How was *Annie*?"

"It was great. I wish you could have seen it with us."

"Maybe we can go someday."

She ran to her room and my mom hugged me.

"How are you?"

"Not good, Mom." Tears started to swell in my eyes. "I'm in love with him."

"Ugh, Brielle. You'll get through this. I promise. You're surrounded by family and friends who love you. Plus, you have that little girl in there and you're her whole world. Don't forget that."

"I know." I wiped my eyes.

"You're better off without him. And to be honest, I'm glad this happened now before you got further involved with him. He's not a good man, sweetheart, and he proved it to you."

"I know."

Stella went over to the piano and started playing.

"I have to go. Call me later," my mom spoke.

"I will. Thanks again, Mom."

I walked over to the piano, sat down next to Stella, and watched her play.

"Why are you so sad?" she asked me.

My daughter was too smart and sometimes I underestimated her.

"Are you sad because of that man at the art gallery?"

"Sometimes adults get sad too, sunshine. Especially when they lose a friend."

"Was it because of me?" she asked as her fingers played the keys.

"No. Not at all."

"He said he wished he never knew you. That was mean."

I pressed my lips against her head.

* * *

Later that day, Sasha came over and took Stella to Central Park while Ben drove me to the shooting range. I was filled with hurt and anger and I needed to release it somehow.

"Long time no see, Brielle," Jimmy spoke as I walked through the door.

"Life's been kind of crazy, Jimmy."

"Are you okay?" he asked.

"Yeah. I'm okay."

I took my bag and went into lane three. Taking out my gun, I loaded it and began firing multiple rounds.

"Damn, Brielle," Jimmy said as the target moved forward. "I get the impression that the target is someone you know. What's going on?"

"Broken heart."

"Aw, gee. I'm sorry." He hooked his arm around me. "Want me to shoot him for you?"

I couldn't help but let out a laugh.

"No. But thanks. If anyone is going to shoot him, it's going to be me." I smirked.

27

ONE MONTH LATER

Brielle

I spent all my days and nights with Stella, and as much as she loved having me around 24/7, she did start asking questions. She asked why I wasn't working anymore. I told her I was taking a break so I could spend more time with her before she started school in the fall.

One afternoon, I decided to go to Kyle's restaurant and see if I could talk to him.

"Can I help you?" the hostess asked when I walked inside.

"Is Kyle Chamberlain available?"

"May I ask who's asking?"

"Brielle Winters."

"Let me go check. I'll be right back."

"Brielle," I heard Kyle's voice as he approached me.

"Hi, Kyle. I'm so sorry for just dropping in like this. I was wondering if I could steal a moment of your time?"

"Of course. Let's go sit down over here. Are you hungry?"

"No. I'm fine. Thank you."

We took a seat at a table in the corner and he had a waitress bring us some coffee.

"So, what's up?"

"I need to know what happened in Caden's past."

"Gee, Brielle. It's not my place to tell you."

"I know it isn't, and if I wasn't desperate, I wouldn't be here asking. Please, Kyle."

"What does it matter now, Brielle? Even if I tell you, it's not going to change anything."

"I know it won't. But I just need to know because I care very deeply for him. If I could just know what happened, I think it will help me move on."

"Eight years ago, Caden was in a car accident. The same accident that took the life of his girlfriend, Cassandra. He received a call from one of her girlfriends. They were at a party and Cassandra had gotten involved with some drugs, so they called him to come get her. When he got there, he found her on the couch making out with some guy. He put her in the car and they got into an argument about the guy and the drugs. It was storming really bad that night, and when Caden was going around a curve, he lost control of the car and hit an oncoming truck. The impact of the accident killed Cassandra instantly, and Caden escaped with a couple of broken ribs and some bruises. He's blamed himself every day for that accident and for Cassandra's death."

"But it was an accident," I spoke.

"I know. But my brother doesn't see it that way. Since that night, he's closed off his entire self to everyone. He put all of his energy and focus into the company. I hated seeing him go through what he did. That accident changed him. He doesn't allow himself to get involved with women romantically. It's just sex, and if a woman wants more, he immediately cuts her off. Until you. I know my brother, Brielle, and he would never pay for sex. I believe he did that with you so he could keep you around without having to admit that he had feelings for you. Despite what you think about him, he's not a bad man. He's just damaged. How old is your daughter?"

"She's six. I should have told him, Kyle."

"Nah. You kept your personal life separate from your business life, and Caden needs to understand that you had every right to."

"I can imagine what you must think of me and my line of work. Caden asked me what kind of person would sell their body when they have a kid."

"I don't like to judge people because you never know someone's circumstances. You're an amazing and smart woman, Brielle, and you're doing what you have to in order to provide for your daughter. I get that and Caden does too. He just won't admit it."

"Thank you, Kyle. I've decided to get out of the business. I'm done with escorting and I'm going to find something else. I'm thinking about taking Stella and moving away from New York and making a fresh start."

"You can always make a fresh start exactly where you are. Don't let my brother and his actions force you away from your family and friends."

I gave him a small smile as I placed my hand on his.

"Thank you for talking to me."

"You're welcome, Brielle. Any time."

We both stood up from our chairs and I gave him a light hug.

"Bring Stella into the restaurant and dinner is on me." He smiled. "I'd love to meet her."

Caden

I spent the last month working more than I ever had, trying to keep myself busy enough so I didn't have time to think about her. Did it work? No. It also didn't help that I sat outside her apartment building and watched her come and go from time to time. The chaos in my head was overwhelming and I couldn't control the thoughts of her and what happened that night eight years ago. Kyle suggested I go to therapy and talk to someone, but that wasn't my style. I had a hard enough time opening up as it was and speaking to a total stranger wouldn't be any easier.

I took in a deep breath as I walked into her building and took the elevator up to the seventh floor. Finding out which apartment she lived in wasn't hard, especially when money was involved. Like I said before, everyone has a price. I knocked on the door, and when it opened, the tiny human was standing there staring up at me.

"Do you always open the door for total strangers?" I asked.

"I looked through the peephole first. You're the man from the art gallery. We talked, so you're not a total stranger."

"Okay. Anyway, is your mom home?"

"She's in the shower. Did you come here to upset her again?"

I furrowed my brows at her.

"No. I came here to speak to her."

"You can come in and wait until she gets out of the shower," she spoke as she opened the door wider.

I stepped inside and looked around. Her place was very nice and as clean as a whistle.

"Would you like some coffee?" she asked.

"Umm. Sure."

She pushed a step stool up to the counter, took down a mug, and poured some coffee from the pot into it. I stood there with my head cocked and stared at her. As she went to pick up the mug, I ran over and took it from her before she spilled it and burned herself.

"Thank you."

"You're welcome. Cream and sugar?" she asked.

"No. Black is fine. What is your name again?"

"Stella."

"I'm Caden. How old are you?"

"Six."

"Is your father around?"

"No. I don't know my dad. My mom said he was a coward and took off when he found out she was going to have me. She said we're better off without him in our lives."

"She's right."

I continued looking around and noticed a baby grand piano

sitting in the corner. I found it odd she never told me she also had one.

"Nice piano."

"Thank you. My mom bought it for me. I'm teaching myself how to play. Music is good for the soul."

"What kind of music are you teaching yourself?"

"Classical music."

"I play the piano too. My mother taught me when I was a child."

"Really?" She grinned. "Can you play something for me?"

"I guess I could." I narrowed my eye at her.

We walked over to the piano and I took a seat on the bench. Before I knew it, she sat down next to me with a smile on her face. I placed my hands on the keys and began to play a Mozart tune.

"Wow!" The smile on her face grew wider.

"It's all in the feeling. You have to feel each note."

"Stella, when did you learn—Oh my God!"

I stopped playing, turned around, and stared at her as she stood there in a black silk robe with soaking wet hair.

"Mommy, look who came over."

"Hello, Brielle."

"What the hell are you doing here, Caden?"

"I thought it was time we talked," I replied.

"Stella, I need you to go down to Grandma's. I'll call her and tell her to meet you at the elevator."

"But, Mommy. I want to stay and listen to Caden play."

"Stella, now!"

"You better do as your mom says. I can play for you again sometime."

"Okay." She huffed as she got up from the bench.

28

Brielle

I stood there in shock as my heart pounded out of my chest. What the hell was he doing here? I picked up my phone and sent a text message to my mom.

"I'm sending Stella down. Can you meet her at the elevator? I just got out of the shower to find Caden playing the piano in my apartment. He wants to talk."

"Jesus, Bri. I'll go to the elevator now. Stay calm."

"Thanks."

"Grandma is waiting for you at the elevator, Stella."

"It was nice to see you again, Caden." She smiled. "Thank you for playing something for me."

"Umm. You're welcome, Stella."

As soon as she walked out the door, I shut it and turned to him.

"Who do you think you are just showing up here?"

"Being as stubborn as you are, I knew you wouldn't answer my call. So, really, I had no choice but to drop by unannounced. Stella seems like an okay tiny human."

"She's an amazing child and highly intelligent."

"She's very polite and well-mannered for a six-year-old. You've done a great job raising her."

"Thanks. I try my best."

I walked into the kitchen and poured myself a cup of coffee. Seeing him hurt my heart even worse than it already was.

"She told me she doesn't know her father."

"Jesus Christ, what else did the two of you talk about?"

"What happened with him?"

"Short version of the story. He got me pregnant and the night I told him, he went out for food and he never came back. I haven't seen or heard from him since."

"It must have been hard on you," he spoke.

"It was at first, but then I realized he did us a favor."

"I agree. How did you escort being pregnant?"

"I wasn't escorting at the time." I took a seat at the table. "I had gotten out of the business when I met Daniel and got a job as a secretary at a marketing firm. It didn't pay much. Certainly not what I made escorting, but I did what I could. While I was on maternity leave, they ended up going out of business and I was left without insurance and a job. After I had Stella, I blew through everything I had saved. I wasn't about to let the cycle repeat itself. A single parent with a kid and absolutely no money to support her. So I got back into escorting. It was fast and easy money and I could give Stella everything she needed and more. So when you asked me what kind of woman with a kid sells her body for money, my answer is the kind of woman who is thinking about her child and wanting to give her the best life possible."

"I get that. I just wish you would have told me about her from the start."

"Why, Caden? What would it have mattered? I was keeping my personal and business life separate. I always have to protect Stella."

"I came here to apologize to you for the things I said. I can't put my mind to rest until I do. So, I'm sorry."

His apology was sincere. It was probably the most sincere thing he'd ever said to me.

"Okay. I accept your apology."

"Thank you. I appreciate it, Brielle. You have a really nice place here. Why didn't you tell me you also had a piano?"

"How could I? You'd want me to play something and I can't play. Then you'd be questioning me as to why I had a piano." I smirked.

"True." He chuckled. "Listen, I should get going. I just stopped by to apologize to you."

As much as I wanted him to leave, I didn't. I wanted to feel his lips against mine again and his strong arms wrapped around me. But I wasn't sure if things could ever be the same again.

"Thanks for stopping by." I softly smiled.

"No problem. I'll see you around sometime."

He walked to the door and placed his hand on the handle.

"You told Stella you'd play the piano for her again. I wouldn't want her to be disappointed," I spoke.

He turned his head and our eyes met.

"Sure. Maybe some time I can. Enjoy the rest of your day."

"Thanks. You too."

The moment the door shut, I felt a sickness in the pit of my belly. It had been a month since I'd heard from or seen him and I thought I was getting over it, but then, seeing him here brought the heartache all over again.

Caden

I climbed into the limo and took in a deep breath. I felt more alive in this moment than I had in a month. She accepted my apology, which was good, but would she truly ever want to possibly see me again after the way I treated her? Shit. I pulled out the card of a therapist that Kyle had given me. It was the same one he saw when he was going through some shit with the company and wanted out all those years ago. Maybe it wouldn't hurt to talk to him just one time. Nobody would ever have to know. Instead of going to his office, Dr.

Carlyle agreed to come to my penthouse for a session. He only agreed after I told him I'd triple his fee if he did. Everyone has a price.

Later that evening at seven p.m. sharp, the elevator door opened, and Dr. Carlyle stepped out.

"You must be Caden," he spoke as he extended his hand.

"Thank you for agreeing to meet me here, Dr. Carlyle. I appreciate it."

"No problem. Who am I to turn down a triple fee an hour?" he smirked.

"Can I pour you a drink?"

"No." He put up his hand. "Water will be fine."

I poured him a glass of sparkling water and then poured myself a double scotch. I was going to need it.

I took a seat on the couch as he sat in the wingback chair across from me. I told him everything about Cassandra and that night and then I proceeded to tell him about Brielle.

"You took the first step with Brielle in apologizing. That was very good, Caden. But I'm going to be totally honest with you, until you forgive yourself for the accident and Cassandra's death, you will never be able to move forward with anyone."

"How can I forgive myself? It was my fault. If I hadn't been driving so fast in that storm out of anger, it never would have happened, and Cassandra would be alive today."

"You don't know that for sure. Forgiving yourself is crucial, Caden." He looked at his watch. "Our time is up. I want to see you at least three times a week until you get a handle on this. How is tomorrow night? Same time?"

"Sure. Tomorrow is fine."

After he left, I poured myself another drink, took it out to the terrace, and leaned over the rail. Talking to Dr. Carlyle wasn't as hard as I thought it would be. In fact, I felt a little lighter. I couldn't stop thinking about Brielle and how I wanted to see her again. But I needed to take baby steps to gain her trust back. Plus, I still needed more therapy.

29

TWO WEEKS LATER

Brielle

I thought after Caden apologized, I would hear from him again. But I hadn't. I picked up my phone dozens of times and stared at his name in my contacts trying to work up the nerve to message him. But I couldn't. If he wanted to talk or see me again, he would have reached out. Maybe his apology was only for him, to make himself feel better. As I was cooking dinner for me and Stella, my phone rang and Caden's name appeared. Instantly, my belly started to twist, and my heart started racing.

"Hello."

"Brielle, it's Caden. Are you home by any chance?"

"Yes. I'm home. Why?"

"Is Stella with you?"

"Yeah. She's here too."

"I was wondering if I could drop by for a bit. I owe her a song on the piano. I mean, if you're not busy or anything."

"No. I'm just cooking dinner. I'm sure Stella would love for you to come over and play for her. She's been asking about you."

"I don't want to interrupt your dinner."

"You're more than welcome to join us. I'm making chicken parmesan."

"I really don't want to intrude. I can come another time."

"You wouldn't be intruding, Caden."

"Mommy, is that Caden on phone?" Stella asked with excitement. "Is he going to come over to play the piano with me?"

"Yes, Stella, he is."

"Yay!" She jumped up and down.

"See, Mr. Chamberlain, now you don't have a choice. You wouldn't want to disappoint a six-year-old tiny human, would you?"

"No. I wouldn't," he chuckled. "I'll be there shortly."

I ended the call with a smile and set my phone down. Walking over to the cabinet, I took down an extra plate and set it at the table.

Caden

Was using her child as an excuse to see her wrong? Probably. But it all came down to baby steps. I'd made a lot of progress with Dr. Carlyle over the past two weeks. More progress than I ever thought would be possible. The car pulled up to her building and I climbed out and took the elevator up to her apartment. After knocking on the door, Stella opened it and startled me when she grabbed my hand.

"Welcome back to our home." She grinned.

I stepped inside and Stella led me to the kitchen.

"Hi." Brielle smiled.

"Hi." The corners of my mouth curved upwards.

"Dinner will be ready in a minute. I hope you're hungry."

"I am. It smells delicious."

"Come on, Caden, let's go play the piano."

"Stella, it's time to eat. You two can play after dinner."

"Aw, Mom!" she whined.

"Your mom is right, you know. We can't play good music on empty stomachs." I smiled down at her.

"We can't?"

"No. We can't."

"Okay." She grinned.

"Is there anything I can do to help you?" I asked Brielle.

"You can pour us a glass of wine if you don't mind." She smiled at me.

"Of course. I can do that."

She handed me two glasses and I poured the wine in each of them. Walking over to the table, I set one down in front of Stella.

"I can't drink wine." She giggled. "I'm not old enough."

"Really? I thought you were at least twenty-two." I winked. "My apologies, Madame."

She continued to giggle as Brielle set the food on the table. We took our seats and began eating.

"I'm going to a new school in the fall," Stella said.

"You are? What's wrong with your old school?" I asked.

"I'm too smart for it. I'm going to the Speyer School for the gifted children."

I looked at Brielle with an arch in my brow.

"Well, you will certainly get a good education there."

"I know and I can't wait." She giggled.

"I can see you get your intelligence from your mother."

"I do. She said that my dad was extremely unintelligent with the brain of a snail."

I let out a laugh as I looked at Brielle.

"Stella, you're not supposed to tell people I said that."

"Sorry, Mommy."

We made small talk while we ate and I couldn't stop thinking about how right it all felt.

"That was really good, Brielle. Thank you."

"You're welcome." She smiled.

"Mommy, can we go play the piano now? Please?" Stella begged.

"I'm going to help your mom clean up first and then I'll play something for you. But why don't you go play and I'll listen as I'm helping to clean up," I spoke as I got up from my seat.

"You don't have to help me, Caden. I got this."

"You cooked, so I can help clean up."

As we were clearing the table and taking the dishes to the sink, Stella went over to the piano and began to play "Fur Elise" perfectly. So perfectly that it sent chills down my spine.

"How long has she been playing the piano?" I asked Brielle.

"About two months."

"Who's her teacher?"

"Nobody. She teaches herself."

"And she's never had a lesson in her life?"

"No. She didn't want lessons. She insisted on teaching herself. She's really good, isn't she?" She grinned.

"Yes. She is. Have you ever had her IQ tested?"

"Her previous school tested her."

"And?" I asked with an arch in my brow.

"150."

"What?" My jaw dropped. "She's practically a genius."

"I know. All I want is for her to have a normal life."

"Sorry to tell you this, sweetheart, but life for her will never be normal."

When she finished playing "Fur Elise," she moved on to a new classical piece, one I didn't recognize. I helped Brielle clean up the dishes and then walked over to the piano and took a seat next to Stella.

"What piece is this?" I asked her.

"A piece I wrote myself."

"Excuse me? You wrote this?"

"Yes. Do you like it?"

"Where's the music sheet?"

"In my head." She smiled.

She finished the song and moved over.

"Your turn."

I stretched out my fingers and began to play a piece by Bach. Stella sat there and watched my fingers while bobbing her head up and down. Before I knew it, she placed her fingers on the keys next to mine and started to play with me. I glanced over at her and smiled.

"That was fun. Mommy, did you hear us?"

"Of course I did, sunshine. You both were incredible. Now I think it's time for bed."

"Do I have to?" she whined.

"Yes. You've had a long day."

"Okay." She pouted. "Is it okay if I say good night to you after I get in my pajamas?" she spoke to me.

"Of course."

I got up from the piano and walked over to the couch where Brielle was sitting.

"She's an incredible kid."

"Thanks. You don't like the tiny humans. Remember?" She smirked.

"True. But I think I might like your tiny human." I smiled.

30

Brielle

"Can I get you another glass of wine?" I asked him.

"You stay here. I'll get it."

Seeing him play the piano with Stella warmed my heart and turned me on. He walked over with the bottle of wine, refilled my glass, and poured some into his.

"I'm surprised you're home this evening. I thought maybe you'd be with a client."

"I gave up the business. I'm not doing that anymore."

"You're not?" he asked with surprise. "Why?"

"It was time. Especially with Stella getting older."

"Good idea." A smile crossed his lips. "Have you decided what else you want to do?"

"I was thinking about starting a real freelance marketing business."

"I think that's a great idea. You're smart and a good business woman. You've already built one successful business on your own, so this should be a piece of cake."

"You think so?"

"I know so."

"I'm ready for bed!" Stella exclaimed as she ran over to us.

"Say goodnight to Caden and get in bed. I'll be there to tuck you in."

"Good night, Caden." She wrapped her small arms around his neck.

"Good night, tiny human." He grinned at her. "Sleep well."

"I will." She giggled. "I hope we can play the piano together again soon."

"Definitely." He gave her a wink.

As soon as I tucked Stella into bed for the night, I walked back out to the living room and sat down next to Caden.

"I've been thinking. I would like to take you and Stella to dinner tomorrow night at Kyle's restaurant. What do you say?"

"I think Stella would love that." I smiled.

"And how about you?" he asked.

"I'd love it too."

"Good. Then I'll pick you both up at six thirty. I should get going. I have an early meeting in the morning."

"Oh, okay."

We both got up from the couch and I walked him to the door. Our eyes locked on each other's as he brought the back of his hand up to my cheek and softly stroked it.

"Thank you again for dinner."

"You're welcome."

His touch made me tremble. A feeling I'd never once forgotten.

"Enjoy the rest of your evening," he spoke as he opened the door.

"You too, Caden."

He walked out, shutting the door behind him. I slowly closed my eyes for a moment as a smile crossed my lips.

Caden

I was on cloud nine after I left her place. The chemistry between us was still there and stronger than ever and I knew she felt it just as strongly as I did. I pulled out my phone and dialed Kyle.

"Hey, bro. What's up?"

"I need to make a reservation for three for tomorrow night at seven."

"For three? Who are the other two people besides yourself?"

"Brielle and her daughter Stella."

"Seriously?"

"Yes. Is that a problem?"

"No. Not at all. It actually makes me very happy to hear you say that. You're down for three for tomorrow night, and you all will be getting the special VIP treatment. I'm happy for you, Caden. I'm truly happy."

"Thanks, Kyle, but it's just dinner."

"Baby steps, bro. Baby steps. And hopefully the first of many."

I smiled as I ended the call.

※

After I left the office, I headed home, changed my clothes, and headed to her apartment. After knocking on the door, it slowly opened, and Stella stood there in her pink dress and bright blue eyes staring up at me.

"Good evening, Madame." I bowed to her. "Are you ready for dinner?"

"Yes." She giggled. "Come in. Mommy's almost ready."

"She's not ready yet?"

She signaled with her finger for me to come down to her, so I knelt down, and she whispered in my ear.

"She wants to make sure she looks perfect."

"Is that so?" I whispered back.

"Yes." She nodded her head. "But I don't think I was supposed to tell you that."

"It'll be our little secret. And for the record, I think she always looks perfect." I winked.

"What are you two whispering about?" Brielle smiled as she walked into the room.

"Nothing. Wow. You look—"

"Perfect, Mommy."

"What she said." I smiled.

"Thank you both very much. I'm starving, so we better get going."

When we arrived at the restaurant, we were immediately seated at a table and I told the hostess to tell my brother that we had arrived. A few moments later, he walked over to our table.

"Brielle, it's good to see you again. You look stunning." He leaned in and lightly kissed her cheek.

"Thank you, Kyle. It's good to see you as well."

"Bro." He smiled as he shook my hand.

"Kyle, I'd like you to meet Stella, Brielle's daughter. Stella, this is my brother, Kyle."

"What a lovely young lady." He grinned as he extended his hand to her. "It's a pleasure to meet you, Stella."

"It's nice to meet you too." She placed her small hand in his. "You look like Caden."

"But I am way more handsome." He winked at her.

"In your dreams." I rolled my eyes.

He sent over a bottle of his finest champagne and a fizzy strawberry drink for Stella. After we placed our order, I excused myself and walked into the kitchen.

"She's a beautiful little girl," Kyle spoke.

"Yeah. She's pretty great. Listen, after dinner, is it okay if Stella plays the piano?"

"What?" His brows furrowed. "We have a full house tonight. I'm not sure my customers want to eat their dinner while listening to a six-year-old bang on the piano."

"She's not going to bang on it, Kyle."

"Not a good idea, Caden. I don't need any complaints."

"Okay. Just thought I'd ask first." I smirked.

After we finished dinner and before dessert, I glanced over at Stella.

"Did you see what's sitting over there?" I pointed.

"A piano." She grinned. "I saw it already."

"How would you like to play something for the people in the restaurant?"

"Caden, I don't think—"

"It's okay, Mommy. I want to play it. Please."

Brielle looked at me and shrugged her shoulders.

"Are you sure Kyle won't mind?" Brielle asked.

"Nah. He won't mind at all."

I took Stella's hand and led her over to the piano.

"What do you want to play?" I asked her as she took a seat on the bench.

"I think I'll play Mozart."

"Good idea." I smiled at her.

The restaurant was noisy with people holding conversations and laughter. The moment Stella placed her fingers on the piano keys and began to play, everyone went silent. I stood there, next to the piano, with my arms folded and a smile on my face.

"What the fuck!" Kyle exclaimed as he walked up from behind.

"I told you she wouldn't bang the keys."

"My God, Caden. She's brilliant."

"I know she is." I grinned. "She has a gift. Mom would have loved her."

"Yeah. She would have. She's better than us."

"Please. We don't even come close to her."

"True."

As soon as Stella finished the song, everyone in the restaurant started to clap. Clapping that went on for what seemed like forever. She stood up from the bench and bowed. I took her hand and led her back to the table.

"You were amazing, sunshine." Brielle smiled as she hugged her.

"Thanks, Mommy. Can we have dessert now?"

"You can have all the dessert you want." I patted her head.

31

Caden

It was late and way past Stella's bedtime according to Brielle. When we stepped into the apartment, she told Stella to go and get ready for bed.

"Thank you for tonight." She smiled. "I had a really good time and I know Stella did too."

"You're welcome." I took hold of her hand.

"I'm ready, Mommy!" Stella came running into the living room. "Can Caden tuck me in?"

"Sure. I think I can do that. I've never tucked a tiny human in bed before, so you may have to show me how."

"It's not rocket science." She giggled.

"Are you sure it's not rocket science?" I scooped her up and she giggled all the way to her room.

I tucked her in bed and tapped her on the nose.

"Good night, tiny human." I smiled.

"Good night, Caden. Maybe you can come over again and we can play the piano."

"I'd like that."

I turned off the light and pulled the door, only leaving it open a crack. Walking into the kitchen, I found Brielle putting dishes away.

"I better get going."

She put the last dish away, turned, and looked at me.

"You can stay," she softly spoke.

I walked over to her and pushed a strand of her hair behind her ear.

"As much as I want to, I can't."

"Why?" She looked up at me with her beautiful blue eyes.

"I just can't."

I traced her lips with my finger before leaning in and softly kissing them.

"I'll be in touch," I spoke as the back of my hand swept across her cheek.

Turning around, I walked to the door and left. The ache in my heart was fierce, but I couldn't stay with her. Not yet. There was something I had to do first.

Two days later

I stopped at the florist and picked up some flowers. Climbing out of the limo, I held them in my hand as I walked across the lush green grass, glancing at the gravestones of beloved ones who had passed away. If I was ever going to free myself, I needed to do this. I remembered exactly where it was, even though the last time I'd been here was eight years ago. I bent down and set the flowers on her grave.

"Hi, Cassandra. I know it's been a long time and I'm sorry about that. I just couldn't bring myself to come back here. I've done nothing but carry around this massive amount of guilt. The kind of guilt that held me a prisoner of my own life. I should have been the one who died that night, not you, and I'm so sorry." Tears sprang to my eyes.

"I'm sorry for everything and I accept full responsibility for what happened. I came here today because I need to forgive myself. If I don't, I can't move on with my life."

I stayed for a while and continued to talk. Dr. Carlyle was right. Talking to her was the first step towards healing, something I should have done years ago. After I left the cemetery, I pulled my phone from my pocket and dialed Brielle. The second step towards healing was to tell her about my past.

"Hello."

"Hi. It's me."

"Hi. How are you?"

"I'm good. Listen, is there any way you can get a babysitter for Stella tonight and come over to the penthouse. I need to talk to you."

"It's already covered. My mom and her boyfriend are taking her to the movies tonight."

"Great. Can you come over around six? I'm planning on leaving the office early today."

"Six will be fine. I'll see you then."

"Looking forward to it. Enjoy the rest of your day, Brielle."

"You too, Caden."

B*rielle*
I set down my phone and held my coffee cup between my hands as Sasha sat across from me.

"What did he want?" she asked.

"He wants me to come over tonight. He said he needs to talk to me."

"Do you think it's bad or good?"

"I have no clue."

My belly twisted in a knot.

"I'm sure it's good, Bri. I mean, just a couple days ago, he took you and Stella to dinner. He wouldn't just flake out now. Would he?" She bit down on her bottom lip.

"You never know with him. You should see him with Stella." I smiled. "It just melts my heart. And she likes him so much."

"But this is the man that hates kids," she said.

"If you want to know my opinion, I don't think he really does. What if he changed his mind and decided that he doesn't want anything to do with us?"

"I don't think that's the case. If that was true, you'd just never hear from him again." She reached across the table and placed her hand on mine. "Relax, sister. Everything's going to be all right. I have a good feeling about this."

"I love him, Sasha, and I don't know what I'd do if he decides me and Stella aren't right for him."

"You're worrying for nothing. But if that's the case, then you're going to move on. You have a company to get up and running." She smiled. "In all honesty, that should be your priority right now."

"I know." I sighed.

We said our goodbyes and I left the coffee shop. Pulling my phone from my purse, I called my mom.

"Hey, sweetheart."

"Hi, Mom. Is it okay if Stella stays the night at your place tonight after the movies? Caden called and he wants me to come over to talk."

"Talk about what?"

"I don't know, but I'm really nervous."

"Judging by the things you've told me recently, I think it'll be a good talk. I really want to meet him, Brielle."

"If all goes well tonight, you will soon."

"Stella does nothing but talk about him, and when she does, there's a light in her eyes. The same light you get when you talk about him. Of course I'll keep her all night."

"Thanks, Mom. I love you."

"I love you too."

I headed over to Stella's friend's house to pick her up.

"Oh, hey, Brielle," Bonnie, Miranda's mother, spoke as she opened the door.

"Hey, Miranda. I'm here to pick up Stella."

"I'll go get her. Come on in."

Stella came running over to me and hugged my legs.

"Hey, sunshine. Are you ready to go home?" I patted her head.

"Yeah." She smiled.

"Go say goodbye to Miranda."

"So," Bonnie spoke, "Stella has been talking a lot about a man named Caden. She told me that you're seeing him."

"Not really. We went out a couple of times," I lied. "It's too early to tell if anything is going to come of it."

"Then maybe you shouldn't have introduced him to Stella so early," she spoke. "If things don't work out that could be damaging to her."

I was ready to tell her to fuck off and mind her own snooty business, but she didn't know me or the whole story."

"I know. My bad." I smirked. "Come on, Stella. Let's go! It was nice to see you again, Bonnie. By the way, how's your husband doing?"

"He's fine. Always working to provide us with the best of everything."

"That's great. Have a good day." I smiled.

"You too."

Little did she know that her husband wasn't "working" all the time. In fact, he'd spent a few afternoons in my hotel room complaining about how his wife didn't meet his needs and forced him to seek fulfillment elsewhere.

As Stella and I walked home, which was only a few blocks away from Miranda's house, I told her that she'd be spending the night at her grandma's house.

"Why do I have to?" she whined.

"Because I'm going over to Caden's house tonight and I don't know what time I'll be home."

"Can't he just come over to our house instead?"

"No. He wants to have a grown-up talk. No kids allowed."

"That's boring. I'm good at grown-up talk." She grinned.

"You are, but tonight is just for me and Caden. You understand, right?"

"I guess." She pouted. "When can I see him again?"

"I'll ask him tonight."

32

Brielle

I stepped inside the elevator, my heart rapidly beating and my palms a sweaty mess. I honestly didn't know what to expect tonight, which made me more of nervous wreck. As soon as the doors opened, I stepped out and saw Caden walking towards me.

"Thanks for coming. Can I make you a drink?"

"Yes. Please. A martini if it's not too much trouble."

"No trouble at all. In fact, I'll make one for myself as well."

I followed him into the living room and noticed all the furniture was different.

"You got new furniture?"

"I did. Do you like it?"

"I do." I grinned. "It's very chic."

"I felt the need for a change." He handed me my martini. "Have a seat." He gestured.

I took in a deep breath before taking a sip of my martini and sitting down. My heart was still racing as I tried to convince my body to settle itself down. He sat down next me and set his drink on the coffee table. When he turned to me, our eyes locked and he took the drink from my hand and set it down next to his. Bringing his hand up to my cheek, he softly stroked it.

"I asked you to come here tonight because there are some things I want to talk to you about. One being about us."

I took in a breath and went to speak, but he stopped me before the words came out.

"Let me finish." He smiled. "From the moment I laid eyes on you back in Texas, I felt like I'd been hit by a bus. And even worse when I saw you out of disguise. I knew right then and there, I wanted you, which you know to be true, since I agreed to pay you seventy-five thousand dollars a month. Which you gracefully negotiated your way to eighty thousand." He grinned. "What you didn't know at the time was that I was willing to pay that just so I could see you as much as I wanted to. I had or tried to convince myself it was only for sex, but it wasn't. It was for much more, but I just couldn't and didn't want to admit it. The more time we spent together, the harder I fell for you. The more I got to know you, the more I fell for you. When I was with you, for the first time in years, I was a happy man and I didn't deserve to be. That's why I got so angry when you'd ask me about my past or if anything was wrong. Everything was wrong. Not with you, but with me." I swallowed hard. "There's something I need to tell you about my past."

"Caden, I already know," I softly spoke.

"What? How?"

"About a month after you found out about Stella and told me you never wanted to see me again, I went to Kyle's restaurant and begged him to tell me what was going on with you. I needed to know because I knew you weren't okay and it bothered me. I guess I just needed to know for closure. I needed to know that it wasn't me you were actually running from. You could say it somewhat soothed the sting of rejection."

"And yet you're here, and you invited me into your home and let me take you and your daughter to dinner. I was so terrified because the feelings I have for you were so strong that I was afraid I would let you down somehow. That I would ruin your life like I did Cassandra's. When I found out about Stella, I was relieved because it was my way out, and not like you think. It was my reason to let you go so I didn't hurt you. But I couldn't let you go. I tried. I really did. Hence the reason for the new furniture."

"What?" I softly laughed.

"You spent a lot of time here and we had sex on various furniture in this room. It reminded me too much of our time together, so I thought if I could bring in some new things, it would ease the pain somehow and make me forget about you."

"Caden." I brought my hand up to his cheek. "What about the bedroom?" I smiled.

"That's all new too. I couldn't sleep in that bed. The scent of you still lingered every single night."

"Seriously? You bought a new bedroom set?"

"I did." The corners of his mouth curved upwards.

He took hold of both my hands and gently squeezed them.

"I'm in love with you, Brielle, and I am extremely fond of Stella. I asked you here tonight because I would like to start over. What I'm trying to say is that I want to be with you and I'm hoping you can forgive me for all the mistakes I made, and you'll say you want to be with me too."

Finally, my heart returned to its normal rhythm and the knot in my belly dissipated.

"Of course I want to be with you," I spoke as tears filled my eyes. "I always have. I love you, Caden Chamberlain."

He closed his eyes for a moment and let out a sigh of relief. Then he let go of my hands, brought his up to my face, and wiped away the tears that were beginning to fall.

"You have no idea how happy I am to hear you say those words, and I promise, I'm going to be everything to you. I'm going to give you my best, and if I ever let you down, I want you to tell me."

"You're never going to let me down. You are a beautiful man, inside and out, and I'm the luckiest woman in the world that you chose me."

He pulled me into him and held my head tightly against his

shoulder. Feeling his arms around me again made me whole and complete. He broke our embrace and brushed his lips against mine.

"How long until you have to be home?" he asked.

"Tomorrow morning." I smiled.

"Perfect." His lips pressed against mine with a smile.

33

THREE MONTHS LATER

Caden

The past three months had been nothing short of incredible. I had never been in love with anyone like I was with Brielle. She was my very existence. The bond between Stella and me grew stronger every day. I loved that tiny human as if she were my own. She taught me things through the eyes of a child. Things I never really saw before. She was an incredible little girl with the dream of becoming a classical pianist/composer when she grew up. But, to me and a lot of others, she already was. She loved to play, and she practiced for three hours every day. She belonged at Juilliard. I had a contact there and invited her over to my penthouse to hear Stella play, with Brielle's permission, of course. Needless to say, she was blown away and offered Stella an audition. Shortly after that audition, she was accepted to study in their pre-college division where the youngest child currently there was the age of eight.

Brielle was out to dinner with Sasha and I stayed with Stella at her apartment. I was growing tired of the back and forth between homes and I wanted both of them to move into the penthouse with me. But there was something I needed to do first. As I sat next to

Stella and listened while she played Bach, I pulled a small box from my pocket.

"Stella, can you stop for a moment. I need to talk to you about something."

"Sure." She smiled as she removed her fingers from the keys.

"I bought this for your mom. What do you think?"

"Is that a wedding ring?! It's so beautiful, Caden."

"It's an engagement ring and I'm going to ask her to marry me. Do you think she'll say yes?" I tickled her.

"She'll say yes." She giggled. "If you get married, that means we can be a family."

"It sure does. But this has to be our secret. I have a plan and I need your help."

"Okay. I would love to help." She grinned.

I told her my plan and she loved the idea. I told her to get ready for bed and I pulled out my phone and called Kyle to set the plan in motion.

"Can we play something together before I go to bed?" Stella asked as she came running over to me in her pajamas.

"Of course we can."

&.

As soon as Brielle got home from dinner, I took her into the bedroom and made love to her. As her head lay on my chest, I softly stroked her hair.

"I was thinking we could go out tomorrow night. Maybe have dinner at Kyle's restaurant."

"I'll have to get someone to babysit Stella," she spoke.

"It's already taken care of."

"What?" She lifted her head.

"Ben's going to watch her. I asked him and he's very excited about it."

"Wow. Look at you." She smiled as she kissed my lips. "I'm looking forward to our date night."

"Me too, darling. Me too."

***

The next day, I could barely work. I was way too nervous about tonight. I knew I didn't have anything to be nervous about, but we hadn't talked about marriage or even moving in together. As I was sitting at my desk, trying to concentrate, my phone rang. It was Brielle.

"Hello, gorgeous." I smiled as I answered it.

"Caden, I just got a delivery at the door, and when I opened the box, there was a stunning dress inside it."

"Oh good, it came already. That's for you to wear tonight."

"It's kind of fancy. Don't you think?"

"Nah. I think it's perfect. Do you like it?"

"Are you kidding, I love it. It's beautiful."

"Good. I'm looking forward to seeing you in and out of it tonight."

"You're bad. What time are you picking me up?"

"Seven. Be ready."

"I will be. Thank you for the dress. I love you."

"I love you too. I'll see you later."

After changing into my tux, I picked Brielle up precisely at seven. As promised, she was ready and waiting.

"Damn, woman. You look gorgeous." I kissed her lips.

"So do you. Are we going to some black tie affair you didn't tell me about?"

"No." I chuckled. "I just thought it would be fun to get all dressed up for the hell of it."

When we arrived at the restaurant, Brielle looked around and noticed we were the only customers in the whole place.

"Why are we the only people here?" she asked.

"Kyle was kind enough to let me rent out the place so it could just be the two of us."

"That's sweet, but why?"

"Why not? I thought it would be nice to have a romantic quiet dinner for two."

"Good evening." Kyle smiled as he stepped over to our table. "I brought a bottle of my finest and most expensive champagne for you both," he spoke as he poured some into our glasses.

"Thank you, Kyle," I said.

"I can't believe you let him rent out your restaurant." Brielle smirked.

"Everyone has a price." He gave her a wink. "Your dinner will be out shortly."

I held her hand from across the table as we talked about her day. Her marketing business was getting off the ground. Of course I had a helping hand in it. But the only thing I did was send one company her way to get her started and things took off from there. I had never been prouder of her.

Kyle walked over and set our plates with the stainless steel dome lids in front of us.

"Since when do you serve your dinners like this?" Brielle asked.

"I do on occasion for our special VIP guests." He smiled. "Enjoy."

I gave him the signal to go get Stella set up at the piano. Brielle went to remove the lid from her plate and I stopped her.

"Wait!"

"What?" She laughed.

"I want to make a toast to us first." I picked up my champagne glass. "Here's to your rising business and the amazing relationship we have together."

"Cheers." She grinned as she tipped her glass to mine.

"Let's eat," I spoke.

I carefully watched as Brielle removed the lid and stared down at the diamond ring that was sitting by itself on the china plate.

"Oh my God!" she spoke.

Just then, the music started to play, and Brielle looked around, taking notice of Stella at the piano.

"Caden." Tears started to fill her eyes.

I reached over, took the ring from the plate, got up from my chair, and knelt down next to her.

"Brielle. I love you so damn much and I love that little girl over there. The two of you have brought so much light and happiness into my world that I never thought I would ever experience. I want to spend the rest of my life with you. I want to love you, take care of you, and help you raise Stella. You are every breath I take and every beat of my heart beats for you. Will you marry me and do me the honor of becoming Mrs. Caden Chamberlain?"

"Yes! Of course I will marry you."

I slipped the ring on her finger and helped her out of her chair, kissing her and hugging her tight.

"You have made me so happy," I spoke.

There was clapping, and when we looked over, Kyle was standing there with a wide grin across his face. The music stopped and Stella came running over.

"Did she say yes?!"

"She said yes!" I smiled as I picked her up and swung her around.

"Wait a minute. You knew about this, Stella?"

"Yes, Mommy, and I told him you'd say yes. Yay! We're going to be a family."

34

ONE MONTH LATER

Brielle

Stella and I were finally settled at Caden's penthouse. He let her pick out the colors for her room and a new set of bedroom furniture. While his piano sat in his study, hers was placed in the living room over by the window that overlooked the city. She was happy to be here and so was I. I had never been happier in my life.

We were in the bubbly filled tub, my back was pressed against his body as his arms wrapped around me.

"There's something I want to talk to you about," he spoke.

"What is it?" I tilted my head and looked up at him.

"I want to adopt Stella. I want her to have my name and I want her to be mine."

"Oh, Caden. I don't know what to say."

"It should be easy since Daniel has never acknowledged her or was ever a part of her life. He abandoned both you and her."

"Yes, definitely. I want you to adopt her and I know she'd love that too. Oh my gosh, she's going to be so excited."

"We have to be married first before we can proceed. So I'm thinking we can move the date of the wedding up six months from now. I don't want to wait, Brielle. I already got in touch with the wedding planner and she's racing for us. That's if you agree."

"Of course I agree. I can't wait to marry you." I smiled. "I'd marry you tomorrow in the courthouse."

"As much as I'd love that, I want you to have the grandest wedding of all time. After all, this will be your one and only wedding."

One Month Later

"Eat your breakfast, sunshine, or you're going to be late for school. Caden, stop distracting her."

"Brielle, please. We're having an intelligent conversation over here," he spoke.

I rolled my eyes as I opened the refrigerator and put the milk away. Caden walked over to me and placed his hands firmly on my hips.

"I have to go. I love you. Have a good day."

"I love you too." I wrapped my arms around his neck as we passionately kissed.

"Ew. Not in front of the tiny human," Stella spoke.

"Then close your eyes," Caden said as he walked over and kissed the top of her head. "Have a good day at school, kiddo. I love you."

"I love you too, Caden."

I grabbed Stella's backpack from the table and we headed down to the lobby. As we exited the building, I froze when I heard a voice from behind.

"Hello, Brielle."

I slowly turned around and saw Daniel standing there.

"Stella, get in the car."

"Who is that, Mommy?"

"Ben, get Stella in the car and take her to school. Make sure you walk her in."

"Of course, Brielle."

"What do you want, Daniel?"

He looked up at the building and slowly nodded his head.

"Looks like you've moved up in the world, Brielle. Is that her? Is that my daughter?"

I stood there, my heart rapidly beating with my hand clutching the strap of my purse.

"I'll ask you again, what are you doing here?"

"I saw in an article where Juilliard accepted their youngest student ever: Stella Winters. I came to meet my daughter."

"It's too late for that."

He glanced down at my finger and saw the three-carat diamond sitting upon it.

"You're married?"

"Engaged."

"It's not too late. I'm her father and I have every right to see her."

"You lost your rights the night you walked out the door and never came back," I spoke through gritted teeth.

"She's my kid."

"She is not your kid." I pointed my finger at him. "Maybe your sperm helped create her, but you are no more her father than any stranger walking down this street. She is happy and well-adjusted and she's thriving. You are not going to stumble into her life six years later and turn it upside down. She doesn't want to meet you anyway."

"How do you know that?"

"Because I told her from day one how you abandoned her. She has a father. A man who loves her and wants to spend time with her, takes care of her, and gives her everything she needs. In fact, he's adopting her as soon as we get married."

"I don't think so, Brielle. She's my kid and I'm not giving up my rights. I came here because I've done a lot of thinking and I want to be a part of her life."

"Why? Because you saw an article and now you think you're going to be a part of the limelight? I have news for you, Daniel, I won't allow you to be in her life, so I suggest you get the fuck back into the hole you crawled out from and leave us alone!"

"This ain't over, Brielle. You can't keep me from seeing her. And if you try, you'll be sorry." He pointed at me as he walked away.

I was shaking as I hailed a cab and climbed in, taking it to Caden's office. When I arrived, I immediately took the elevator up, and his secretary, Louise, told me that he was in a meeting in the conference room.

"Tell him it's urgent, Louise. I need to see him now."

She picked up the phone and dialed the conference room.

"It's Louise. Can you please tell Mr. Chamberlain that Brielle is here and it's urgent?"

Within a couple of moments, he was in his office.

"Are you okay? What's going on?" He lightly grabbed my arm.

I stood in front of him as the tears fell down my face.

"Brielle, what happened?"

I swallowed hard.

"Daniel is back and he wants to meet Stella. He said he wants to be a part of her life." I cried as I placed my hands on his chest.

"What? When did you see him?"

"It was right after you left for the office. Stella and I walked out of the building and were walking to the car when he stopped me. I put Stella in the car immediately and made Ben drive her to school. He told me he saw the article about her getting into Juilliard and now he wants to be in her life. I don't trust him, Caden, and I don't want him anywhere near her."

He wrapped his arms around me and pulled me into him, holding my head against his chest.

"It's going to be okay, darling. I have the best lawyer in New York. I'll call him right now."

He broke our embrace, pulled out his phone, and dialed his lawyer. After speaking to him for several minutes, he ended the call.

"We have a meeting with him tomorrow morning at ten o'clock."

"Okay. Thank you." I wrapped my arms around his waist.

"I don't want you to worry about this. Everything is going to work out in our favor." He kissed the top of my head.

35

Brielle

After I left Caden's office, I went to the shooting range to blow off some steam. Shooting always made me feel better. He said he didn't want me to worry, but I couldn't help it. There was something different about Daniel. I could see it in his eyes. I loaded my gun and began shooting at the target. Six rounds done and I quickly reloaded my gun and began again. I brought the target closer and studied the bullet holes. All perfect shots.

When I was done, I picked Stella up from school and headed home, keeping my gun safely tucked in my purse. Now it would be with me everywhere I went. I wasn't going to lie. I was scared. Scared for Stella.

Two weeks had passed since I saw Daniel and I prayed that he'd given up and left town. Unfortunately, that wasn't the case.

I dropped Stella off at my mom's apartment for the day while I went shopping with Sasha. Caden had called and wanted to go out to dinner, so I told him that I'd meet him at the restaurant instead of going home since I was already close to there. We planned to meet at six thirty, and I arrived at six thirty-five. I was surprised when I didn't see him because he was never late. As soon as the hostess seated me at our reserved table, I pulled out my phone and called him. After a few rings, it went to voicemail.

"Hey, honey. I'm at the restaurant. You must be stuck in traffic. Call me as soon as you get this."

I waited another ten minutes and there was still no word from him, so I sent him a text message.

"Where are you? I'm starting to get worried."

It was now seven o'clock and he wasn't here, nor did he respond to any of my messages. A bad feeling crept up inside me. Something wasn't right, so I called his driver.

"Hey, it's Brielle. Is Caden with you?"

"No. I dropped him off at home and he said he was going to take a cab to the restaurant because I had a family emergency. He isn't there?"

"No and I can't get ahold of him."

"He's probably stuck in traffic and on the phone with a client."

"Maybe. I'm going to try again."

I dialed his number and it rang and rang until voicemail picked it up. My heart started racing, and I knew if I called Ben to come pick me up, it would take too long. I left the restaurant and hailed a cab. A sickness fell into the pit of my stomach as the driver pulled up to the curb of the building.

"Carson, have you seen Mr. Chamberlain this evening?" I asked the doorman.

"Yes. He walked into the building around five forty-five. Is everything okay?"

"We were supposed to meet for dinner, and I can't seem to get ahold of him."

"Well, I know the repairman is up there."

"What repairman?" I nervously asked.

"For the alarm system. He said that there was an issue with your system and he needed to fix it. I called Mr. Chamberlain to let him know and he said to send him up."

"What did he look like?"

"Gee. Umm. He was about six feet tall. Short dark hair. He was wearing a uniform and a hat. He had a scar above his eye. That I noticed right away."

"Shit. I need you to do me a favor and call the police."

"Why?"

"Because the man you described isn't a repairman and I think Mr. Chamberlain might be in danger."

I took the elevator up to the floor below the penthouse and used the stairs the rest of the way up. Approaching the front door, I pulled my gun and my key from my purse. I was shaking with fear as I carefully slid the key into the lock and slowly unlocked the door. Carefully pushing it open, I could hear Daniel's voice. It was coming from the living room. Taking off my shoes, I set them down with my purse, grabbed my phone and took the back way from the kitchen. Holding my phone, I pushed the voice memo button and started recording. I looked around the corner and saw Caden sitting on the couch, his head bleeding, hands tied together, and staring at Daniel, who was standing a few feet away and pointing a gun at him. My rapidly beating heart pounded out of my chest as I raised my gun and walked into the living room. Caden's eyes widened and Daniel turned around.

"What's going on here, Daniel?" I asked as I slowly walked towards him.

"Well, well. Look who's home and thinks she's being a hero. It's good to see you, Brielle. I was disappointed when I got here and found out you weren't. Now be a good girl and put the gun down."

"No way. What are you doing here?"

"Having a little chat with your boyfriend. The man who stole my daughter from me, and the man who's going to pay me a great deal of money to skip town."

"Is that why you came back? For money?"

"Damn right. I used Stella as an excuse because you always had a soft spot for me. I figured if I could convince you to let me meet her, I'd show you how much I regretted walking out on her and then I'd have an in with you and you'd have no choice but to help a troubled man out. But you had to play hardcore and refuse to let me meet her. So, technically, this is all your fault, Bri."

"What kind of trouble are you in?"

"Long story short. I got involved with some bad people after I walked out on you. The Cartel, to be exact. Maybe I shouldn't have stolen all those drugs from them. I owe them a lot of money or they're going to kill me."

"They're not the only ones," I arched my brow at him.

"You're still as cute as ever. I want one million dollars transferred to an offshore account immediately. Once it's done, I'm out of the country. I'll disappear, and I promise you that you'll never see me again. I know your boyfriend is worth billions, so a measly million is nothing to him. Right?" He cocked his head at Caden.

Caden didn't say a word. He just stared at him as Daniel continued to point his gun. I needed to think of how to get out of this situation and there was only one way.

"Put the gun down and Caden will wire the money," I spoke.

"You're crazy, bitch. I ain't putting this gun down. But I do suggest you lower yours. You got some balls handling a gun, but I don't think you have balls to shoot me. The way I remember it, you were always such a fragile little thing. But if you do, your pretty little boyfriend will get a bullet popped in his head."

"You didn't know me like you thought you did, asshole," I spoke as I slowly circled around him.

"Oh, I knew you, Brielle."

"No, you didn't." I arched my brow. "You had no idea who I was when you met me."

"What are you talking about?"

"It doesn't matter now. How do you expect him to wire the money when you have his hands tied?"

"Simple. You're going to do it for him." He smiled.

"And how do you suppose I do that when I'm pointing a gun at you?"

"You're going to be a good girl and put it down. In a matter of minutes, this could all go away. Trust me."

I let out a laugh. "You think I'm going to trust you? I trusted you to be there for me when I told you I was pregnant with your child, and you couldn't do that. What makes you think I'd trust you now?"

"Well, if you want your boyfriend dead, I can arrange that."

"You son of a bitch," I spoke.

"Just to show you how serious I am, I'll wound him for now," he said as he cocked his gun.

Without even the slightest hesitation, I cocked my gun, aimed it at his leg, and pulled the trigger. He screamed as he dropped to the ground, and the gun hit the floor and went off.

"You bitch!" He grabbed his leg.

He went to reach for his gun, and I ran and kicked it out of the way. Suddenly, the elevator doors opened, and several police officers came running in with their guns. I set mine down on the table and ran over to Caden.

"Are you okay?" I took my hand and wiped the blood that was dripping from his head and fiercely untied his hands.

"I'm fine, Brielle. My god, he could have killed you."

We wrapped our arms around each other and held on tight.

"Ma'am, what happened here?" the officer asked.

"That man came into my home with a gun, threatened my family, and demanded we wire a million dollars to his offshore account. I have it all recorded on my phone. It's over there on the table."

The paramedics came in with a stretcher and I walked over to Daniel and knelt down beside him.

"You shot me!" he screamed. "Get away from me!"

"You're lucky I didn't kill you. I could have shot you right in the heart and I wouldn't have missed. But the more I thought about it, death would have been too easy for you. You're going to wish I would have killed you, because what you're going to get in prison will be a hell of a lot worse and I'm going to be there with a smile on my face enjoying every minute of it."

"Get this crazy bitch away from me!" he shouted.

"Ma'am, I need you to step over here," the officer spoke as he held my phone in his hand.

He listened to the entire recording as I stood next to him and another paramedic tended to Caden's head wound.

"This is all the evidence we need. We're also going to need to take your gun. You do have a CCW license, right?" His brow raised.

"Yes. I certainly do."

"Good. This is a case of self-defense. One of our detectives will be in touch. All we ask is that you don't leave town until he does."

"We won't, officer." I spoke.

"Sir, you're going to need stitches. We can take you to the Emergency Room."

"It's fine. I'll take a cab," Caden said.

36

Brielle

Caden sat on the edge of the table and I held on to his hands.

"I was praying that you wouldn't come home," he spoke. "The minute the elevator doors opened, he hit me over the head. I had no idea it was him."

"How could I not come home? You didn't show up to dinner and I kept trying to call you. I'm so sorry. This is all my fault."

"Stop it. Don't say that. None of this is your fault. He's a deranged lunatic, but I'm happy you chose not to kill him." He brought his hand up to my cheek.

"Why?"

"Because I don't want you living with someone's death on your hands for the rest of your life."

The doctor walked in, and while he stitched up Caden's head, I tightly held his hand.

Once the elevator doors opened, we stepped into the foyer and then into the living room, where a puddle of blood stained the large area rug that sat on the floor. We both stood there, hand in hand, and stared at it.

"I never liked that rug anyway," he spoke.

"It was okay, but I totally would have picked something different."

"Shall we go shopping tomorrow for a new one?" he asked.

"Yeah. I think we should."

We slowly walked up the stairs together, changed out of our clothes, and climbed in bed, holding on to each other as if our lives depended on it.

"How are we going to explain to Stella the hole in the wall where the bullet from Daniel's gun hit it?" I asked.

"We're not. We're going to pack a bag tomorrow morning and stay at the Plaza Hotel for a couple of days while it's being fixed. I'll get a crew out here first thing. We'll make a special day of it. Just the three of us."

"I like that idea." I smiled as I kissed his lips.

"Listen," he spoke as he stroked my cheek. "It's okay to break down. I know you're feeling the effects of what happened tonight, and I don't want you to hold it in."

I stared into his eyes and swallowed hard as the tears started to fall. He tightened his arm around me as I laid my head on his chest and sobbed.

*

Five Months Later

I stood in the room at the church as Sasha fixed my veil.

"There. Now you're ready." She smiled.

"You look so beautiful, Mommy."

"Thank you, sunshine."

The last five months were extremely busy planning the wedding, filing the adoption papers, running my business, court dates, and trying to put what happened behind us. The best was yet to come and that was all I focused on.

"Are you ready? Your groom is waiting for you at the altar." Sasha smiled as she handed me my bouquet.

I met Ben at the back of the church and hooked my arm around his. The music began to play. Sasha walked down first and then Stella followed, throwing rose petals down as she made her way to Caden.

"Are you ready?" Ben smiled at me.

"I'm more than ready."

We slowly walked down the white runner and I couldn't take my eyes off Caden as he stared at me with a smile on his face. When I reached him, Ben took my hand and placed it in his.

"You are absolutely stunning," Caden spoke with a tear in his eye.

"So are you."

Our ceremony lasted about thirty minutes, and after I slipped the ring on Caden's finger, the minister pronounced us husband and wife.

"You may kiss your bride, Caden."

The smile on his face grew wider as he leaned in and we shared a passionate kiss.

"By the power invested in me, I give to you Mr. and Mrs. Caden Chamberlain."

Everyone started clapping as Stella ran over to us and Caden bent down and picked her up. The three of us walked up the aisle together as a family. Once we reached the doors of the church and stepped outside, Stella placed her small hand on Caden's face.

"I love you, Daddy."

"I love you too, my beautiful daughter," he spoke as he hugged her tight.

Our reception was held at the Waldorf Astoria, where approximately four hundred guests attended and celebrated our special day. It was elegant and the type of wedding I'd always dreamed of. What made it even more special was when Stella composed a song for us for our first dance has husband and wife. Her and Caden arranged the entire thing and kept it a secret from me until he took my hand and led me to the dance floor. I was in awe of this once damaged man who opened up his heart and let us inside. I loved him more with every day that passed, and I made sure that I told him.

"I love you so much," I softly kissed his lips as we danced.

"I love you too and I always will." He smiled.

For our honeymoon, we spent one week alone in Aruba and then Caden flew my Mom, Steven, and Stella to Hawaii, where we spent another week together.

One Month Later

Caden was still at the office when Kyle and Mercedes dropped off their baby Zachary. I agreed to watch him so they could have a date night. It had been a long time since I watched a baby and I was pretty excited about it. I was in the kitchen preparing a bottle for him as I held him, when Caden walked in.

"Hi, darling," he spoke as he kissed my cheek. "Hey there, Zach." He smiled.

"How was work today?" I asked him.

"It was good. Very productive."

I took the bottle and Zachary and sat down on the couch to feed him. Caden sat next to me and stared down at him as he sucked down his bottle.

"You look really sexy holding that tiny human," he spoke. "Maybe we should have one of our own."

"Really?" I smiled at him. "You want to have a tiny human?"

"Yeah. I do. We never talked about having kids and I think we should. How many do you want? I mean, in addition to the one we already have."

"Maybe one more? I think two is a nice number. But I'm not ready to have one just yet."

"Oh. Well, me either. I was just throwing it out there and letting you know that I'm all for having another child running around the house."

"Maybe in a year or two?" I said.

"Sounds good to me." He smirked.

After Zachary finished his bottle, I burped him and then he started to scream. I walked around with him and patted his back, but he wouldn't settle down.

"What's wrong with him?" Caden asked.

"I don't know. He ate, he's been changed. I guess he's just fussy."

"Here, let me see if I can get him to quiet down."

I handed him to Caden, and he still screamed his head off.

"He hates me," he spoke.

"No he doesn't. He's just fussy."

"What's Zachary crying about?" Stella asked as she walked into the living room.

"We're not sure, sweetheart," Caden replied.

"What's wrong, tiny human?" Stella softly spoke as she took hold of his hand.

Instantly, he stopped. Caden and I looked at each other. Then he started wailing again.

"I think I know what he wants," Stella said as she walked over to the piano and started playing. The moment he heard the music, he settled down.

"Get his bouncy chair, quick," Caden spoke.

I grabbed his chair and set it next to the piano. Caden put him in it, and as Stella played, he fell asleep.

Caden hooked his arm around me.

"We'll have it made when we have our own tiny human." He kissed the side of my head.

EPILOGUE

TEN YEARS LATER

Caden

"How do I look, Mom?" Stella spoke as she walked into the kitchen.

"Simply gorgeous."

I narrowed my eye at her as I stared at the short dress she was wearing.

"Is something going on tonight that I don't know about?" I asked.

"I'm going on a date, Dad."

"With whom?" I arched my brow.

"His name is Kevin."

"How old is this Kevin kid?"

"Twenty-one." She grinned.

"Over my dead body! Get back upstairs! Brielle, did you know about this?"

Both of them started laughing.

"Relax, overprotective father. He's sixteen. He goes to Juilliard and he plays the violin. I think you'll like him."

"Oh. Okay then." I narrowed my eye at her.

"He's here!" she excitedly spoke as she ran to the elevator.

"I'm not ready for this, Brielle."

"She's sixteen. She's done concerts at Carnegie Hall. She's played with the New York Philharmonic, and she's a straight A student. She deserves to have some fun. Plus, she's at that age."

"That's what I'm worried about. What kind of fun are they going to have?"

"You're so adorable when you're stressed out." She kissed my cheek.

We walked into the living area and Stella introduced us to him.

"Mom, Dad, this is Kevin. Kevin, these are my parents, Brielle and Caden."

"It's nice to meet you both." He extended his hand to us.

"It's so nice to meet you, Kevin." Brielle smiled as she shook his hand.

I stood there and narrowed my eye at him as I lightly shook his hand.

"Stella tells us that you play the violin," I spoke.

"I do. It's always been a passion of mine since I was a child. Stella tells me that you also play the piano."

"I do."

"Mom, can you help me pick out which purse to take?" Stella asked.

"Of course, sweetheart."

The two of them went upstairs and I used this opportunity to have a little chat with Kevin. I hooked my arm around him.

"So, Kevin. What are your intentions with my daughter?"

"Excuse me, Mr. Chamberlain?"

"What are your plans for tonight?"

"We're going to go to dinner and then come back here and play some music if that's okay with you. Stella and I have been working on a project. We're composing a song together."

"Hmm. Okay. Sounds like a fun evening. You do know to keep your hands to yourself, right?"

"Yes, sir. Of course."

"Dad, what are you doing?" Stella asked as she walked back in the living room.

"Kevin was just telling me your plans for this evening. You two have fun." I patted him on the back with a smile.

"Come on, Kevin. Let's go." She grabbed his hand.

I cleared my throat and he immediately pulled his hand away from hers.

As soon as the elevator doors shut, Brielle turned and looked at me.

"Really, Caden? It looks like you scared that poor boy to death."

"He's sixteen, Brielle, and his sex drive is kicking in at high gear."

"Well, don't worry. I already had the talk with her, and she told me that she is nowhere near ready to have sex yet."

"She's sixteen. All sixteen-year-olds lie. Remember what you were like at sixteen?"

She stared at me as she bit down on her bottom lip.

"Shit. I always lied to my mom."

"Exactly." I pointed at her.

She hooked her arm around me and laid her head on my shoulder.

"Let's go make some martinis and check on the twins," she spoke.

"Good idea, darling. Good idea." I sighed as I kissed her head.

ONE NIGHT IN PARIS

CHAPTER ONE

Anna

Each of my bridesmaids gave me a hug and left the bridal room to go take their places. A few moments after they left, there was a light knock on the door, and when I opened it, my best friend, Franco, stood there holding my veil.

"Your veil." He grinned as he stared at me from head to toe. "You look absolutely beautiful, Anna."

"Thank you. Get in here!" I smiled as I pulled him inside the room.

I stood in front of the three-way mirror and stared at my reflection.

"You really outdid yourself with my wedding dress," I spoke to him.

"You deserve only the best, Anna." He smiled as he placed the veil he made on my head. "Are you okay?"

"Yeah. I'm fine."

I walked to the balcony and stared out at my future husband waiting for me with approximately two hundred guests who had properly taken their seats.

Franco took hold of my hand and lightly gripped it as he stood next to me.

"You don't have to do this. There is always plan B."

"I know. I better get down there. I'm late and my dad's going to kill me."

He let go of my hand, held out his arm, and walked me to the back of the hotel and down the stairs, where my father waited for me.

"You're late," my father spoke as I took hold of his arm. "That is disrespectful to Matthew and your guests, Anna."

"Franco had to fix a button on my dress. It came loose."

The music started to play, and I took in a deep breath. My stomach was tied in knot after knot walking down the white runner as every single guest stared at me. This was what was expected of me. But the thing was, I was never good at doing the expected. I stared at my future husband as he stared back at me. Even his stare was annoying. We were almost to the end of the aisle when I came to an abrupt stop. It was now or never. I chose now.

"I'm sorry, Dad," I spoke as I turned to him and placed my hand on his cheek.

"Anna?"

I turned around, kicked off my heels, and ran up the aisle, throwing my wedding bouquet behind me with a smile on my face. I heard both my father and Matthew shouting my name, but I ignored them and kept running. I ran up the steps, into the hotel, through the lobby, and out the front door, climbing into the black limo that was parked along the curb.

"So you did it." Terrance, my driver smiled.

"I did it. Thanks for waiting for me."

"Not a problem, Anna. Airport?"

"Yes." I smiled.

Freedom and exhilaration soared through me as the plane took off from LAX. I was on a high. Something I always got when I was defi-

Chapter One

ant. I was a strong-willed, independent woman and when someone told me to do something, I always did the opposite. I'm not going to lie, Matthew wasn't the love of my life. Why did I accept his marriage proposal? Because it was what my father wanted. I thought for once I'd grown up and I could make him proud. He brought Matthew into the company to groom him and to run it with me one day. That was how we met. He was practically shoved down my throat every single day and he was persistent about taking me out. So I finally gave in and went on a date with him. He was good-looking, and the rest is history. He grew on me, but I wasn't happy at all. I just went with the flow, worked, and planned my wedding. The way he kissed my father's ass was annoying. In fact, everything he did was annoying. Even the sex with him was annoying. I faked more orgasms than I had real ones. I gave myself better orgasms than what he could give me.

The plane touched down in Paris, and as soon as I turned on my phone, there were numerous text messages and missed calls from my father, with the exception of one text message from Franco.

"I knew you'd do it. Call me when you get to Paris, regardless of the time."

I took a cab to the Peninsula, where reservations were made for Mr. & Mrs. Matthew Bondi. Yep. I did it. I took our honeymoon anyway. I loved Paris and I needed the escape.

"Bon jour." The man behind the desk smiled.

"Bon jour. Reservations for Bondi," I spoke.

"I'm sorry, Mrs. Bondi, but that reservation was cancelled yesterday."

I rolled my eyes. "Of course it was. And for the record, I never became Mrs. Bondi. I left my fiancé at the altar and I'm still Anna Young. So, since my honeymoon suite was cancelled, I'm going to need a room. The Garden Rooftop suite if available."

"I'm sorry, Miss Young, but that suite is booked. I can put you in our Katara Suite that's right next door."

"The Katara Suite will be fine." I smiled.

"Very good. I'll have someone bring up your bags."

Chapter One

I took the elevator up to the sixth floor, and as I was sliding my keycard to unlock the door, I noticed an incredibly sexy man walking out of the Rooftop Garden Suite next door.

"So you're the one who took my suite." I smirked as he passed by.

"Excuse me?" He stopped and turned around.

"Nothing. It was a joke. I just flew in and I wanted that suite and they told me that it was already booked."

"Well, we could always share it if you want it that badly." A sly smile crossed his perfectly handsome face.

"I'm sure your wife wouldn't appreciate it."

"I'm not married."

"Oh. Well, then your girlfriend wouldn't appreciate it."

"No girlfriend either. It's just me in there."

"I'm good with this suite but thank you for the offer." I blushed.

"If you change your mind, you know where to find me. I need to run. I'm late for a meeting." He smiled.

I sighed as I watched his six-foot-two stature and fine ass walk down the hallway in his tailored designer dark gray suit that fit him perfectly in all the right places. His brown hair was kept short all the way around with a slightly longer top, which had a wavy texture to it, and his rich brown eyes were captivating as they held me in a trance. In fact, every feature on his face was captivating. Damn, that man was sexy.

I opened the door to my suite and stepped inside with a smile on my face.

"Welcome to Paris, Anna," I spoke as I looked around.

***

I hope you enjoyed the first chapter of One Night In Paris. To read more, click the Universal Amazon link below!

getbook.at/OneNightInParis

BOOKS BY SANDI LYNN

If you haven't already done so, please check out my other books. Escape from reality and into the world of romance. I'll take you on a journey of love, pain, heartache and happily ever afters.

Millionaires:

The Forever Series (Forever Black, Forever You, Forever Us, Being Julia, Collin, A Forever Christmas, A Forever Family)

Love, Lust & A Millionaire (Wyatt Brothers, Book 1)

Love, Lust & Liam (Wyatt Brothers, Book 2)

Lie Next To Me (A Millionaire's Love, Book 1)

When I Lie with You (A Millionaire's Love, Book 2)

Then You Happened (Happened Series, Book 1)

Then We Happened (Happened Series, Book 2)

His Proposed Deal

A Love Called Simon

The Seduction of Alex Parker

Something About Lorelei

One Night In London

The Exception

Corporate A$$

A Beautiful Sight

The Negotiation

Defense

Playing The Millionaire

#Delete

Behind His Lies

Carter Grayson (Redemption Series, Book One)

Chase Calloway (Redemption Series, Book Two)

Jamieson Finn (Redemption Series, Book Three)

Damien Prescott (Redemption Series, Book Four)

The Interview: New York & Los Angeles Part 1

The Interview: New York & Los Angeles Part 2

Rewind

One Night In Paris

Perfectly You

Second Chance Love:

Remembering You

She Writes Love

Love In Between (Love Series, Book 1)

The Upside of Love (Love Series, Book 2)

Sports:

Lightning

ABOUT THE AUTHOR

Sandi Lynn is a *New York Times, USA Today* and *Wall Street Journal* bestselling author who spends all her days writing. She published her first novel, *Forever Black*, in February 2013 and hasn't stopped writing since. Her addictions are shopping, going to the gym, romance novels, coffee, chocolate, margaritas, and giving readers an escape to another world.

Be a part of my tribe and make sure to sign up for my newsletter so you don't miss a Sandi Lynn book again!

Facebook: www.facebook.com/Sandi.Lynn.Author
Twitter: www.twitter.com/SandilynnWriter
Website: www.authorsandilynn.com
Pinterest: www.pinterest.com/sandilynnWriter
Instagram: www.instagram.com/sandilynnauthor
Goodreads: http://bit.ly/2w6tN25
Newsletter: http://bit.ly/2Rz0z2L

Printed in Great Britain
by Amazon